Bill Dixon

Dragonfire

A New World
of Poems
and Stories

authorHOUSE®

AuthorHouse™ UK
1663 Liberty Drive
Bloomington, IN 47403 USA
www.authorhouse.co.uk
Phone: 0800.197.4150

Published by AuthorHouse 10/17/2017

ISBN: 978-1-5462-8356-0 (sc)
ISBN: 978-1-5462-8355-3 (e)

The dragon who thought he was God.
Always went to bed very late
For the measure of the World
Was his pan-dimensional fate

He was always last to bed,
And the very first to rise.
For the furred and feathered kinder
Had to be a standard size

He had laid down very strictly
Codes and rules and regulations
Measured weights and standard colours
On designs for his creations

Travelling light with dark foreboding
Up the downs of Salisbury,
Down the sugar mines of Castor,
By the shores of Battersea.

Always probing, scrutinizing
On the laws that he'd laid down.
Birds were primed to sing the praises
Of his hypothetical renown.

His obsession, like all good ones,
Started in his cradle days
For his slightest wish was granted
Proof-positive of Godlike ways.

Many tried to reason with him —
He treated logic with disdain.
For he had a will of iron
In a Neanderthal brain.

His proud and haughty Mother,
By nature calm and wise,
Tried repeatedly to cure him
With bitter scorn and sweet advice.

Always full of female wiles,
She never lost her temper,
Except in January, March,
And May through to December.

She had argued with conviction,
Erudition and panache. –
'Gods not red, four feet tall,
And dousn't eat coal and hot ash'

The dragon sulked, shuffled his feet
And muttered in vexation. –
'Drexyl' – that was his name
'Try excommunication'

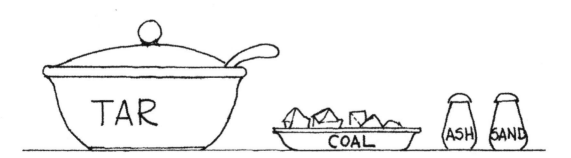

His doctor a Griffin of great eminence,
Was clinical, logical, neat.
But all of his cases were diagnosated
By studying maps of their feet

Footologist extrordinare
Author of that mighty tome
'Feet of infamous and famous -
Feet at work, and feet at home.

He argued that though hard to prove,
And difficult to refute,
And harder still to quantify
(Unaided by square root.)

He doubted that the Lord of All,
The one who calls the shots,
Went around as Drexyl did
Tying young damsels to rocks.

Drexyl merely said that he
Was travelling incognito -
"For on the lesser planets
Its the only way to go!'

The doctor sadly shook his head
And muttered in his chin
'This dragon takes me for a fool
Thats no cognito hes in.'

He thought it an unusual case,
Interesting but not gripping
And suggested as a remedy
That its talons needed clipping

It was very hard work being God.
Serving judgments cataclysmal.
Moving mountains, damming rivers,—
And the hours were so abysmal.

But in the evening, after supper
Sipping cups of relaxation.
He would muse in rosy humour
'I've a job with satisfaction'.

But pride leads surely to a fall,
And fate was playing bad luck poker.
Slyly dealing from the bottom,
Ace, King, Queen and then the Joker.

So, picture if you will the scene,
As in a field of clover lazes
Our hero, who with pen and ruler
Checks on clover, grass and daises.

An idle glance he casts aloft
To see the clouds go skipping by.
Then horrorstruck gasps at the sight,
Theres a mistake in the sky!

The sun is shining as ordered,
Pre-ordained for the afternoon.
But in the heavens darkling quarter,
Floats a pale and ghostly moon.

Drexyl gasped and caught his breath,
With effort he fought back the terror.
At four-oclock in the afternoon,
The moon had made a greviouserror.

Drexyl the dragon was fuming with anger.
He was bubbling, frothing, steaming with ire.
He flung himself upon the ground
And belched forth orange balls of fire.

With an effort superdragon,
And rising to his fullest height.
He proclaimed in voice stentorian
Enough to put the moon to flight.

But the moon still hung before him.
Ignoring all his puff and bile.
Shining brighter with each minute
Jaunting with a mocking smile.

Quick decisions were needed to stop it.
Decisive actions of minutes not hours.
Drexyl decided without hesitation
To call upon his strongest of powers.

This frightening gift he'd found by chance,
It was his greatest prize.
With ease he made things disappear
By closing his all-seeing eyes.

Using now this awesome power,
This hateful sight was banished.
But when he oped his wondrous orbs,
The loony moon was unvanished.

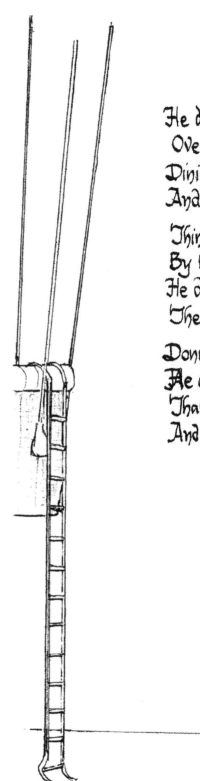

He decided to review the problem –
   Over a meal to calmly take stock.
Dining on charcoal lumps and hot tar
And rock cakes of real rock.

   Thinking that his powers were weakened
   By his distance from the sphere.
He decided to get closer –
   Then the moon would disappear.

Donning all his flying clothing
   He clambered into the balloon
That he kept for cloud inspections
And drifted off towards the moon.

It was higher than he'd thought of
Up amongst the isobars.
High above the tallest mountains
Above the clouds towards the stars.

Gradually the world grew smaller
And larger grew the errant moon.
Till floating calm above the surface
Was Drexyl in his moon balloon.

He was surprised at its largeness,
`At least three miles across' he judged
`This of course explains the reason
That from its point it wont be budged!'

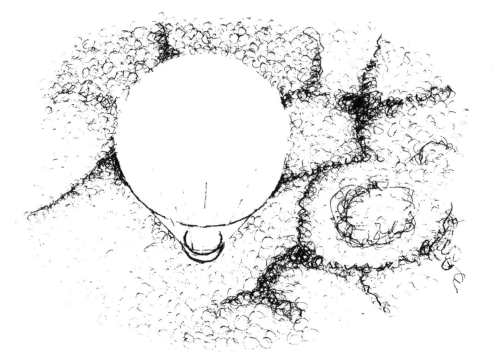

But as he reached its northern pole,
He saw the most amazing sight.
A rope was fastened to the ground
And rose into the infinite.

Drexyl thought 'this isn't usual
Theres a joker in the game
The moon is hanging like an apple
Who's the one to take the blame?'

He could feel his anger rising,
He could feel his hiring ire.
Snorting down his fearsome nostrils,
He roared forth a searing fire.

His ultimate weapon scorched the ether,
The rope began to rip and snap.
Puffed with pride the dragon puffed,
But then alas, he sprung the trap.

The weave of space was ripped apart.
For with a deafening peal of thunder
And with the light of seven suns,
The stars were swayed and rent assunder.

Then from the blackest hole of space,
Unknown, unfathomed and untrod
A shape swooped down upon the scene,
It was the hand of God..!

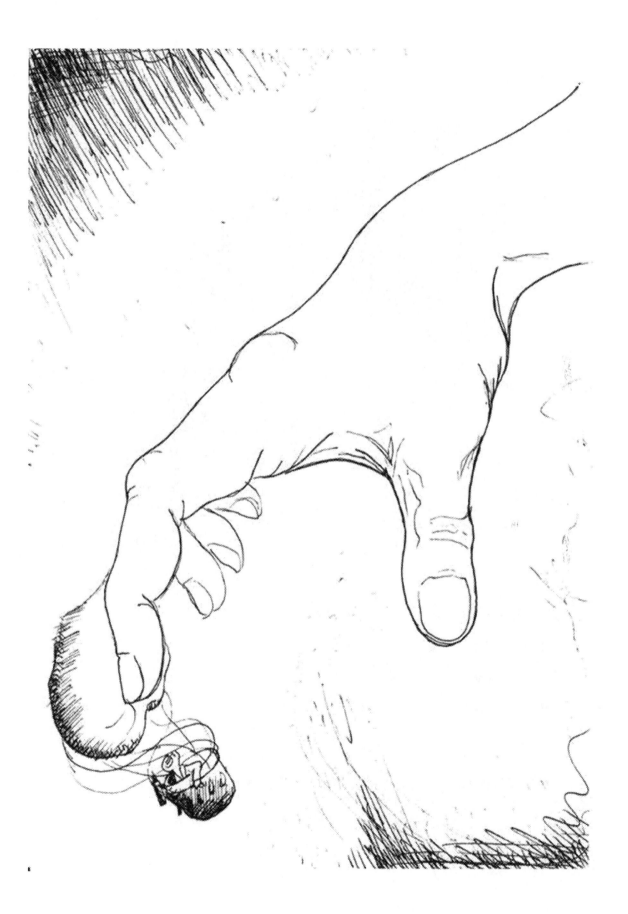

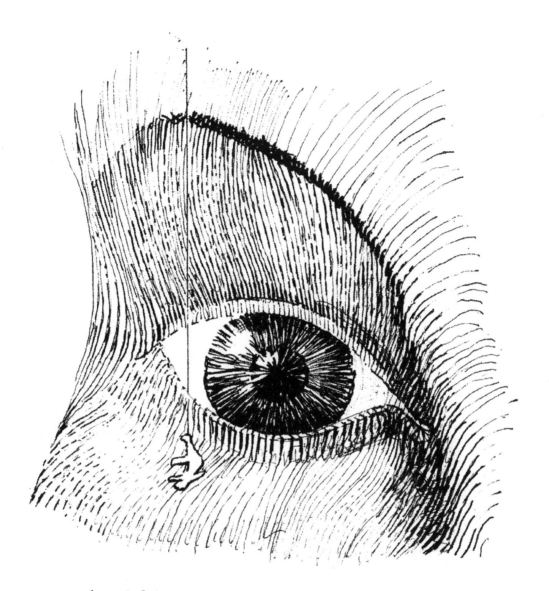

Drexyl twirled slowly in Gods hand.
His face assumed a scornful frown.
But the effect was rather spoilt
Since he was hanging upside down.

God found Drexyl very funny.
And laughed at him with force atomic.
For the design of all the cosmos
Prove Gods nothing if not a comic.

God was always on the lookout
For objects funny, cute or twee.
And viewing Drexyl with amusement
Thought he qualified for all three.

Then she clipped him on her bracelet
Between her other good-luck charms,
The Scurilous of Lapeis Magna,
The Pontifax of Rigatalms.

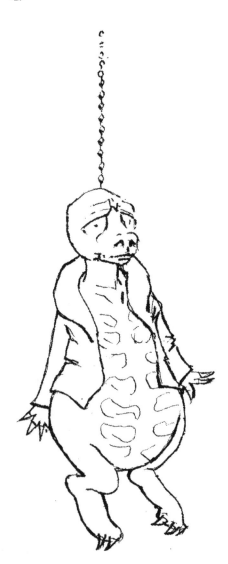

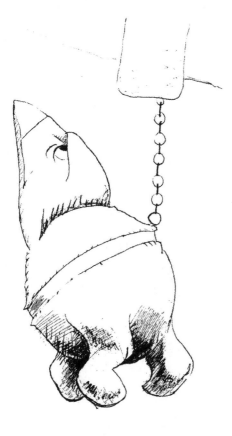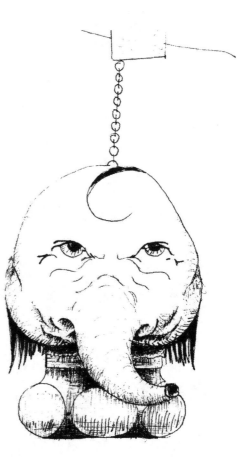

And there he hung in contrite splendour
An oddity amongst the odd.
A curio of the curious,
A worry bead of God.

So be you Dragon, Human, Satyr.
Heed our stories pointed moral.
Never think your God on Highness
For you do so at your peril.

Then the dreaded fate awaits you
That you'll join that troubled band
That jingle-jangle on the bracelet
Of God the Humorists left hand.

ANALOG

A COMEDY

The magic of twilight had come to the city, the colours had drained away to a blue monochrome, the buildings were defined in silhouette and the yellow lights shining out from the windows were welcoming, showing evidence of life in a silent, eerie world, the mist of gloaming roamed the narrow streets. The pub stood on the corner of the street in a drowsy suburb of the city, it was late unspoilt Victorian and very popular due no doubt to its choice of beers and convivial atmosphere. This evening the upstairs room was full with the monthly meeting of the Storytellers Club, the genre had become very popular over the last few years, the room held about eighty and was full, and with a bar the atmosphere was warm and comfortable, the bar and adjoining stage ran down one side of the room with tables and chairs on the other it had a slightly musky, dusty atmosphere, it was quiet, sedate and respectable, in fact disciplined, no one drank too much like a real writer, all were welcome to come on the stage and tell a story, a tale had just been finished a follyfablefull of witches, dragons, peasants and riddles, the usual mythic stuff.

The compere looked on his running list and called on the next teller to tell;' A newcomer with his first story ever, give a warm club welcome to Carl', the usual ripple of applause greeted the man. The man was short, very short, completely dressed in black including a black baseball cap, he was plump and aged about fifty. He slowly mounted the stage, sat on the storytelling chair and removed his cap to reveal a shaven head shining in the spotlight, on the forehead just above the left eyebrow was a black hieroglyph 'h' and above that again in black a ribbon of bar codes and numbers that ran completely round the skull, he had dressed himself well for the part. And as he sat sipping his glass of dark red wine surveying the scene he seemed tense but quietly depressed, for all the world like a Jesuit who'd just found God, he spoke.

'Welcommen!', his voice was low and just about audible.

'My nomus is Truthmaster Drak, Gran Hi Poppadom of the Universal Truth Company and the Granseer Lordus and of the Truth Party, he paused for effect.

I come to you back from the now to tell you the tale of Analog,… shittun star Hartsatease Analog, the man who spoke in riddles, a mythmaker in our law, he broke the Lordus law, he is our greatest dogbreath deviant and danger as all madmen are, he threatens the reason of the city. He made the law bend and sweat with the fire of smith forging fraud, fabricating doubt in our iron truth. And this is not a fiction but a true tale of gross importance to us, we have need to find the truth within the lie and break the code', he was speaking louder with a gutteral accent, like South African and pronounced the word 'break' with a brutal emphasis, it was an important word. The audience was amused and interested, the startling start had been brutally rapid, aggressive and very well acted though so far incomprehensible, the room became silent, drinking became secondary, Drak continued.

'My true story starts one yarn ago and one hour after the dark had ended, the Lordus Light is by now high in the gunmetal sky gilding the city in a golden grey and Analog prepares himself for the day ahead, for his first call to the Truth Kort. He has unhooked from his stem portal, finished his grey meal out of his grey bowl with his grey spoon for there is only one colour and that is grey, what reason for another?, and that's the truth,' Drak slapped his hands together to emphasise the word.

'I tell you Analog was a gross important dude, an intellectual savant he said, to our misfortune he is now a dead intellectual savant and in that is our defeat and his victory'------his voice was louder now, and the tone seemed to be of bitterness and despair, he had his elbows resting on his knees with his hands clasped and was looking at the floor through his fingers,-----' He has tricked and dribbled through our grid we can't solve the mystery in Analog but know the riddle answer lies hidden in the past, he was a pastmaster and clever as a clown, We can't break his subtle code, we broke the key when we broke him, now all we have is shattered foolishness, he was a mirror and is in fragments in our hands. Our world is based on certainty and we always know the truth, with unresolved fact we're lost, for the book demands solution. Should one of you undesigned find the answer I am allowed to offer you release from this your dangerous life to our world of peace and certainty, so try hard, try very, very hard, this is the most important night of you're tearful life, you can be the first immigrant to paradise. The solution is hidden in the pastime and in your infidel irrational world.'

Drak was standing now swaying slightly and had to use the chair as support, breathing heavily he drained the glass. Agitated he ranged around the audience as if someone knew the answer to the question he hadn't put but was perversely holding it back waiting to hear the prize

'*I sing the song of Analog literati dominus, the warrior of the word.*

I am more than cute, more than clever, I'm Intelliger I think about things, I find problems, sometimes where they don't exist, I tell thee I am a fundiment.

For many yarns I have worked on History, as a Seer I have access to all the records, for in Histology we find the truth by logic, all absurdities are amended. In the beginning was the Word and the Word was a lie, verily the truth will out for protohistory is propaganda, myth on mendacity, the ridiculous on rubbish fables and farce, amateurs and assholes, bibles, carnage, democracy, epochs, fools, generals, heretics, idiots, judges, kings, legions, murder, nightime, orgy, prophets, questions, religion, stories, ufter, vice, war, ...and I purify it all by the application of reason to false records, and delete where necessa so that history is as clean as a whisper, as pure as the shriven snow I tell thee I am probably the only one left who knows the meaning of snow, I am a general in the war of the words and lie in ambush for ambiguity so that I slaughter the unterversion and only veracity is the last man standing, What a smartars I am and my nomus is Doktor Analog, yea I am an 'A' an alpha, and a degree man.

Today, for the prima time I've been called to the truth kort to take a reading, I call it Judgment Day, I don't know why I bother, it's a joke for me alone, to laugh in silence and tis woeful in a woeful world. There's no such thing as a joke, there's no such thing as judgement with now, without lies there's no crime to judge and no delight, we all live by the realbook, and the dullness of perfection and that's the truth, for truth is dull, and talking to myself forever more fardles me. But mine readout will result in an upreach to Veracity Proffesori and access to all archives where the dead men live shrouded in lies centuries thick, digging through the dusty layers of virgin records with the archaeology of the word, the treasures are endless, work for a thousand yarns the truth will open up for me and Granseer Lordus will notice and be pleased, Lordus, Lordus, Lordus Amen.

The room was silent now and Drak had seated himself again, he was composed, he was lonely in a room of strangers his hands around another glass of wine, staring wide eyed at the floor he was locked in the story which he seemed almost too tired to tell, a child started crying at the back perhaps from fear and this irritated him. 'We're born to consciousness full grown, complete, no snivelling child invades Utopia' the child stopped, again he spoke.

'Analog's living unit was in Veracity Tower 42336, unit 8, his block was like every other unit, two stories tall, grey and windowless for there is no reason for windows and that's the truth, each room was the standard square six by six with the standard spyeyes in each, it was correct. Over the past half yarn I've been there studying the space and the man who lived there, the room is standard two pod, the room is grey and calm and studious, the décor is the past, peopled by the dead with dead language framed on the walls, he used paper, the old, dead way, he loved the dead you know. The video wall functioned but was unviewed he had stuck some papers on it, and also there was a drape, a banner, probably an old flag hung up in a colour that wasn't grey it also had a symbol in one quarter of it very similar to our own truth ikon, an obvious deviant copy, some of the papers had ancient writing on them, others had pictures showing unknown people dressed as clowns performing shouting songs, the room exuded his rubbish. Above all it is like an exhibit and silent as the grave, you could hear the dust settle. It is correct, nothing out of place, as blameless as the book, so right it's wrong, it contains nothing but arty farty talkwerk, I have a nose for these things and can smell a fartist ten donks away. As a Truthmaster I had called for his examination, for he was an A list and they always need the rackattack, they're clever and powerful with too much knowledge and he had cartloads of knowledge, they think too much, they need stretching. I find too much info fogs the brain and leads to overload and doubts, we in the brutish D class have no doubts and are not fit to understand them for they only talk to each other in riddles, but with the aid of the machines I would break him. Eventually with Granseer Lordus help the sniggering A list would be deleted and replaced, and the universal truth would be closer, or so I thought.' He stopped and held up his right hand in front of his face, he turned it to show the back, then clenched it into a tight fist, he viewed it under the spotlight as if he'd never seen it before, no one spoke, only Drak.

'We have his scan before he left and he was confident arrogant and optimistic, we know he was a deviant and had a stem bypass some longtime in the past. We know they don't contact each other directly but are run as singles by the black machines, they are extreme devious, and only the break clears them but with Analog he wasn't broken, he was self smashed, a self death, suicide, a ruin of the truth. Analog left his unit and went across the city on the A trax, it was a journey without worry or incident as it always is in our city, he was monitored all the way, he did nothing and spoke to no one, all this we know, for we know all.

The vera-city, our world is designed by our machines on a uniform block design with reason ruling all, the blocks are all the same and the spaces between are all the same, variation leads to second best, so every identical block is standard building grey and two floors tall, we live a standard life, we are not layered, no one above, no one below the humblest F lives as the highest A, all people are designed the same and all pods are designed the same, we live a life of certainty and peace. With a city constant temperature inside and out of 46t, we have no rain, indeed no weather, no vegetation, no animals for there's no reason for them and that's the truth and the perfect city goes on for ever and ever, machine designed, uniform, a grey honeycomb always the same, there's no centre, certainly no edge, truly a world without end.

It was a big shop, 1700sq.ft. he proudly used to say, and it was the end of the day. The staff had left, Patrick counted the money, checked the windows, doors and lights twice, switched on the alarm, triple locked the doors and then went in again, he wasn't sure he'd switched off the fire in the office, but he had, so he left. He was at peace with the world, business was good and he enjoyed the taste of life as he walked down the arcade towards his car, he thought about the bright night yet to come.

This was to be their second time out and was important, the first had been to see film which had been O.K., neither had really liked it, a compromise choice, safe, middle of the road chosen so that talk was limited and not to deep, they had got on well considering they were incompatible (male and female).

She was a teacher of arts and crafts and though he ran a shop it was a model shop which needed crafts, and also his desire and obsessions was for art, he practised, performed and studied it in all its forms. They had met at a writing class and though Mo was better than him they appreciated each other

He walked out of the arcade into the town square, and stopped to buy a 'Big Issue' from the seller, he always did this when he wanted good luck for some thing, a propitious offering for the night ahead. Though he was a pragmatic atheist he had certain rituals he practised that helped to smooth things out, there was only one more hurdle and he would be sure of a good result; he must be the last one on the car park, his car must stand alone, so he walked rather slowly to the corner from where he could see the park. It was the worst result, there were three cars left and he felt gutted, he slowed his walk and then stopped, looked down at his shoes, put down his case and carefully retied his laces, opened his case and checked the contents. He stopped to look in a shop window which provided a reflected view of the cars and waited, then the situation changed, a late shopper ambled towards a small red car opened the boot and loaded in his bags. Patrick's heart was lightened, the night would be o.k. he knew that two cars left meant that disaster had been averted so that though he would have to work at it the odds were even, he thanked the god he didn't believe in.

But at the start it didn't seem to be working out too well, as he drove home his mind wandered on to the evening ahead he turned left onto the high street and clipped a parked car. It wasn't a bump, nor a ricochet, more a glissade, very slight, he looked in the rear view mirror the car was empty. He stopped and made a decision, he got out and walked back to have a look, the car was empty with a child seat in the back and a scratch on the rear wing. He walked back to his car got in and waited and watched but nobody came, after ten minutes he had to go he was running late, he wrote his details on a half sheet of paper and sellotaped it to her windscreen, he didn't want it to blow away, he thought it was a girl driver because of the child seat and it was parked badly, The rush hour traffic was heavy so he was even later, he had a shower and shave, put on a new shirt, his smartest suit and a tie, he rarely wore a tie but felt the need to get her approval and not let himself down, she was important. He looked at his watch and relaxed, he was back on schedule, time was important to him and he always liked to be ahead of the game, always arriving a few minutes early so that he was in charge, he now felt good about tonight. He relaxed, made himself a coffee, switched on the radio and draped himself over the expensive leather settee, he rested his head on the arm and drifted seamlessly off to sleep, it had been a long hard day.

Mo had left the school a little earlier than usual and had gone home to have a long wallow in a hot bath and think about things, women like to soak and think, men like a quick shower, her life was drifting, she was in a rut. The school work was predictable and dull and her writing was good but not enjoyable, in fact her whole life was predictable and dull She splashed the water and looked down at her body, she spread her legs, she was loosing it, it just looked like a female body not her body. She could exercise and loose weight, but she'd just look like a thin old women. She was forty and her life was over, she would try not to take it out on men, she closed her eyes and floated in the warm and scented world, free of gravity and all the pains of womenhood floated away, she was floating away in life, helpless over the waterfall ahead. She thought probably she was starting a depression, it felt like it. Drinking made her more depressed, sex made her more depressed, they were always predictable and anyways she was loosing her looks, it was definitely a bugger. She wiped the steam from her glasses, took a sip from her glass of white and considered life, should she give up the struggle and become a comfortable middle aged woman with hobbies. She was after all a mother and needed a rest from multi tasking and standards, the occupation of being a slut was becoming appealing, Tracy had taken to it and was enjoying life with abandon, her vacuum had broken a month ago and she survived. Downsizing was an option, she had always wanted to live on a barge, yes a gypsy life was attractive and she could probably write a book about it, she cheered up a bit.

He felt very happy, for life was perfect as he lay in bed, it was early morning and gazed at her with wonderment, how had he got so lucky?, he kissed her cheek softly and sighed. Everything was perfect since she came and he wallowed in contentment, oh happy man!

There was a sudden bang on the radio and he was wide awake, bloody hell he was late, he was never late, she'd kill him he grabbed the keys and his jacket, switched off the radio and sprinted to the car. He then found he was wearing his slippers, shit! The omens had been right, it was going to be a terrible night

'Through the darktime I had flaked out well, for my partner Lapis Ardmania is a dreamaker and installed my favourite for role downplay, the story of King Bush the fourth and of his triumph gainst the infidel Chin with Tex's golden horde. He fought the heretic with logic, burning out the alien invasion in the tenth war of the cyber years..................... I was for the day full prepared, I felt at liberty to the prospect of recognition and promotion, I was ferocious to fame with all its good times beckoned, like power and glory, like position and status awaited me on this my Judgement Day, for my Intelliger and grasp of veritable data was triumphant, There comes a time in the affairs of 'A' lists when glory comes and sits upon your shoulder as perchance when Caesar crossed the Rubicon, Garibaldi's telescope, Gates with the first machine, we are all touched by the Lordus truth and yea we prosper. So I set out for my reward in the finest fettle, there was no reason for haste, my slot on the Traxus would consign me to the Kort at the exact hour, I always travel alone, talk to no one, I was content, there was no reason to worry for The Party has deleted worry, and that's the truth. Surely I know the future from the working on the past, I'm a pastmaster, Lordus and the party have designed the future for us, and we are designed for improvement, that's the truth.

The city was its usual calm, contented self, beautiful in its myriad pulsating greyness, the Lordus light shimmered in the pearl grey sky, warm and comfortably serene in its wonderful design, it hummed with purpose and I am a person of import in such schematics, designed for glory. The Partyposters on the blocks were showing the truth current to the day, together with the Granseer Lordus as she spoke from the Book of Reason, the periusual mornlight shone on my journey, it was a lollipop day, all was pleasance with me. For I have a secret pleasure with myself alone, a secret in my reasoning that gives me edge in motiva, so that wherein all life, people, city, the whole predicted world are designed for peace, and so designed for sameness and for nothing, and nothing contents me not, my cogitostimularess comes by escape into the past where I can talk forever to the dead, there they can lie and dissemble the world away, and that's my secret truth, my freedom is to live in the past, for there is safety in the past, where I am free to handle lies and catch the disease and enjoy the blessed contagion.

My favor is in the archivation of the songbook halls where all emotion rages through the ages in the danger and the havoc of the word, where there is no truth, only feeling. The words compressed to fit the line talks to me down the time so that I understand and weep in joy. I gluton in the outland talk, each line a spyder web of lies most beautiful, they spy on life and dissect it with the word. I save them in my bypass vaults, a secret deep block universe heaped with the pleasures of the past, the past is my salvation.

The word is all, the thought is all, I tell thee what delights I have to come, drunk on the word and pissed up every darktime, O lucky, lucky man, lucky thrice blest Analog crowned with lies.

I had not seen the Truth Kort before, but I had knowledge from the records, it compassed a complete block and was still only two stories tall but was nine, nine, eight floors deep (we don't count, only machines count, but we know numbers) and that's the truth. The entrance to the block was the full height and two zero donks wide across the top was writ the famous trubook legend 'THE TRUTH WILL SET YOU FREE', the building was a light grey.....we have two, zero, zero shades of grey, and was busy in a calm, measured way with all peoples from 'A' to 'F', and Kort flunky's all dressed In dark grey, almost black, creating a soft staccato murmur of sound, in fact a place of predictable business. The traxus came into the building and curved down to the floor of a hall, I had arrived upon my time affirmed sure. The hall covered the entire block and was coloured white (The lightest grey) and with an intense white light from the ceiling it was difficult to tell where the walls ended and the floor and ceiling began, the light was of a strength to hurt, I shielded mine eyes and almost closed them, for the first time in my life I felt pain and it troubled me. I noted the Kort officials had eyeshades construct er... grafted onto there eyebrows, a bio design for their guild alone it was truly an alien world, surgical and unsafe. I realised I would be scanned as I crossed the gate, my character and position would be known pronto, and then I saw a black garbed figure standing by the postern, it approached me, it was Drak'

He was quieter now and viewed the room with a leery sardonic eye for the drink was strong, he adjusted his position and belched, he felt comfortable.

'I feel you need to know how we made our pureformed city from your sinful world, how has perfection come from dross?, for only then will you understand my problem, the simple answer is design. When Granseer Lordus formed the Truth Party she pronounced her first truth which was that all institutions, discoveries, functions, countries, politricks, movements, religions, in fact the whole mess of your civilisation, of your life, was ruined by you the people you are built to ruin. The D.N.A. the construct of the people was programmed to lie and cheat and maneouvre in every walk of life, so that the fatal flaw in humanity from your beginning would spoil everything until your end, every law you make you bend, you cheat in every sport you play, you despoil every country you discover you have not got the word. He paused to catch his breath, he'd spoken rapidly and with passion 'In the beginning was the word and the word was a lie', your first social instinct was the untruth, as soon as you could talk you lied, you couldn't recognise or know reeltruth to literally save your life. She discovered you were designed for evil and cruelty, you had evolved to singularity desire, to push the door to ego lust, homo sapiens had reached a dangerous dead end, it was obsolete.

So that the first problem to tackle was yourselves, to redesign you, to outake the shit. With the aid of bio-lectronics we designed us, using reason and truth we perfected new humanity both physically and mentally and a new genus was born, we improve and then we clone, we only desire to serve the truth. To ask what Analog looked like, he looked like me, we all look like me, we are all one donk tall, grey in colour and with no body hair, for there is no reason for hair and that's the truth '(he clapped his hands to emphasize)' and with our zip code and nomus gravured around the brow we are instantly readable, we are machine read. We also have two bio implants at birth, a camera in the chest just below the neck (he pulled down his shirt to show a large unblinking eye)and a biodock into the brainstem in the back of the neck so we can couple to the mother, designs for perfect surveillance from the start to termination, In this time you are remote watched, in our time we watch ourselves, for via the machines we self record, and our third eye never sleeps, there are no secrets and all are watched, even myself a master in the delete squad is not beyond inspection, we are designed for the rule of reason and any faults are observed and adjusted. Lordus, by intelligent design created us in self regulating perfection,' Homo Reality'.

It hadn't gone too bad, he was only five minutes late and she wasn't ready, he sat on her settee and talked to her through a crack in the bedroom door about his choice of a restaurant and her suggestion that they went on afterwards to a storytellers club which was often amusing and you could pick up some useful storylines, sometimes she read one of her own. He went along with it but it sounded bloody dull, all fairytale stuff with damsels and dragons, it might not be too bad after some wine with the meal and a relaxing drink in the club.

Her flat was stylish, calm, neat clean and tidy, everything his wasn't, the walls were a beigy colour and hung with prints, not mass produced furniture store nothings but one off hand made art prints, there was one wall of books and a work station with a grey computer and a chrome silver anglepoise lamp, he was impressed and a little intimidated. there was also a long low glass topped coffee table, a kind of hessian covered settee with a woolen 'throw' over the back and a beigy persion cat And then when she came in the room he warmed to the idea, she looked great, she hadn't tried too hard but she looked great, her hair was beautifully brown and the frock matched it, the only problem was it was kind of beigy so that he felt if she leant against the wall she would disappear, but he warmed to her, she was his type of women, strong, he liked a woman to have a strong personality and be intelligent so that she almost dominated him, she was the right height, a bit shorter than him, plump, pretty and well built in a feminine way, very, very pleasing, she lit up the room he kissed her cheek with reverence, she smelled good

'I followed Analog across the city, as a Truthmaster I had ordered his correction for he was guilty. As expected he spoke to no one and contacted no one, we are all alone cocooned in our safety and sanity, it was the normal journey in the city, he was confident in his intellectual 'A' list arrogance, he was as sure as sin. The blinding light in the capture area unsettled and irritated him as it does all who are called, he was out of the grey zone. He was not used to discomfort and looked around for someone to voice a complaint to and tell about his importance, it was then that he saw me, he could see I was a 'D'. I spoke first before he could complain.

"You are A96402279H?" I said

'You know I am, I'm Hartsatease Analog seer in the Histological faculty and require to know why there's no one of quality to meet me, someone of equal status, our Kortruth policy needs correction when such as I am full ignored, why is there no star chamber for high poppadoms?, do you realise I am called in for raising and my power will be ominous. Beware me 'D' I am a high life and nobody's fool at reason's table"

I am hear to meet you, my nomus is Truthmaster Drak, welcommon.

There is obviously a machine cock up in my files, this is a squatdata input, do you not realise how important I think I am?, I am an 'A' and desire, no demand signifysence, consult someone in high degree forthwith and sort this receptor fault before you are in shitruth, I am the future, the chosen and after my advancement I will have you taken apart and amended down to an 'F"

'I was originally an 'F', my nomus was Fear before I joined the brotherhood'.

'You aren't qualified for a high level readout, the contact is malformed, we can't converse as equals cerebral, our language is unphased, you're a base design without the skill, a lumpen prole, a peasant, a 'D' for dunce and A's don't talk to 'D's. I am an A design and only talk with A, B's, the only result you will obtain is default bafflement and head stress, someone of high degree impatiently waits for me upon the stroke, my

slot is late and a machine search spans the kort I am important and you will pay, you will go down, speak the rune or pay the tune, otherwise I will include me out'.

'I will escort you to your truth kort and we will talk'.

'I signalled to two intimidation gards to closecupple with the prisoner and we walked to the descendors, all the way Analog squawked his innocence and I was silent with the truth.

The kort was on level seven, five, eight, so it took five mins to godown, you must remember the deeper the kort the deeper the crime. It is still blindingly bright at these depths and Analog was now showing signs of wear and worry and I was in my element, the thrill of total power in purity was satisfaction good. The kort gard was ready at the gate and she was magnificent, like all gards she towered above us, one donk twenty tall dressed all in black with black boots, black trousers and shirt, a voluminous black cloak, the usual black shades inserted over the eyes, black lipstick and when she smiled, shiny black teeth. She stepped forward to greet me, and I identified the prisoner as Analog

Number A96402279H, and for the first time mentioned his crime 'Machine Deviant star grade', she said "The 'A' list tribe are unworthy of the thought but they are brittle" and then read out the standard indictment.'

'This is kort seven, five, eight of the truth kort.

You have been arraigned to appear before this kort as a deviant and you will pay the price immutable,.

The inquisition will be performed by the correction guild under the supervision of Truthmaster Drak

The inquisition is not for us to test the evidence, we know the truth, it is for you to hear the sin and know the truth.

Today is the start of your new life and glory in the way of the light, you will be made again.

I hereby hand you details of your misdeeds, itemised with dates and times and with the names of informers and your own surveillance data for you have supplied your guilt.

Study this for you have the right to appeal any part of it now, but I would advise you against such a dangerous remedy, to challenge the guilds true evidence will only show the depths of your depravity and you will be immediately transported to level nine, nine, nine'.

Drak looked out over the audience, now the story had got to his speciality he was more relaxed, almost languid, he sipped his wine and acknowledged it was good, better than the Veracity Gin back home.

'Of course you must realise that we are a caring Kort and that our sole aim is the amendment of the prisoner to the light, he (or she) is in default and all impurity must be deleted, we know everything and the sooner the prisoner knows this and that argument or lying are useless, the better for them, to protest against the truth only affirms their guilt. We pride ourselves on the rapid throughput of cases but the 'A' list are usually the longest, they think and talk to much, we have our targets, and the pressure process is applied until the break and reality is reached, to us the break is all, its standard procedure. You undesigneds most great problem is set to in the Lordus first and primal quote 'What is the truth?' which you can't answer for your life's a living lie. The answer is 'The Book Of Truth', you haven't tasted the comfort of reeltruth, a life without worry and with certainty in everything, and a life where resistance and argument is futile against absolute power'. Granseer Lordus has designed our serene life of unquestioning order.

Drak paused for a moment, 2o give you some idea of our methods I have brought with me the summons handed to Analog, I will hand it round for your inspection and awe, for the truth is in the detail.' (herein appended) ....

It was midsummer and still bright daylight as they strolled towards the restaurant, a warm Italian evening he thought to compliment the food and wine. He'd chosen the place with care, it was authentic, with the tables lit by candles stuck in old raffia covered wine bottles, just like Lake Garda, and authentic Italian musac and waiters, you knew it wasn't real but you could pretend through half closed eyes and play the game of make believe. It was his favourite place, make believe and had been since childhood, when he had found the new discovered land, a hideaway where problems vanished and wishes were granted, safe and sound and true. He liked to live there as much as he could, away from the worries and responsibility's of the business and life in general, in make believe he was in control (he liked to be in control of himself) and happy with himself, for that was the secret, to like yourself. He was happy with the night, it was going just as he'd planned.

'I knew the vibes were wrong as soon as I entered the Truth Kort, it was an immense hall, the vast roof unsupported by pillars so there was no place to hide, with many persons inside and entering the concourse, but no one leaving, there was an invisible one way valve in operation, Vero it was a sternfocus on fundiments and no one smiled, it felt efficient, it was a cold concentrated camp, Drak met me at the gate, it was obvious this was his world, pride and power oozed from every pore, he knew I was guilty and I knew I was lost, the only question was the degree of mine crime. I huffed and puffed and bluffed my way along playing on my status and his lowgrade but in this building he was the alpha and I was the omega. He motioned two goongards to my side and with this trinity of dirt I was escorted to the lower depths of this palace with hopelessness as my companion and fear by my side. But I was an alpha and sure with my quality I could operate damage control, first I had to find mine crime and admit it, I had to find the truth, with my brain my only resource, resistance was useless for the truth will out.

The journey on the large descendor was sordid, some prisoners were manacled and deleted, the musik was loud and true, the light was painfully bright, the atmosphere was quiet desperation, nobody spoke but some were crying and some were pissing in their boots. We arrived at the kort and the design of the kort gard was classic, a large black image of unbending power and truth she had a purity that dominated the room, she read out the summons and her voice was clear and bell-like, she was perfect. After the readout I was led into a small cubicle with two chairs, one large with clamps, one small and comfortable, I was clamped into the large one, Drak sat in the other, the two goons remained standing behind Drak and the gard left, then the interrogation started.'

Drak ripped open a bag of crisps with unnecessary fury and eat them with a loud satisfying sound, the salt and vinegar was good, not a grey taste. And although there was no reason he also liked coloured food, it was a devious thought but he craved some comfort, he smiled.

'The purpose of this preliminary is for you to confront the truth, to realise your fault then I can continue with your amendment in the reality room. You see Analog we are both after the same result, we are both after purity and we both have problems, yours is the word, mine is you, An 'A 'list problem is always the same, you are clever, soft and flexible, you're job is dealing with untried material which you have to cleanse. to purify and you intellectuals always have problem with the truth, the rules are clear, any illogical fact is not a fact and leads the way to lies, or perhaps you think there's two equally valid paths to the truth, Analog there's only one path and one truth, we aim for the beautiful simplicity of the one truth, where there are no problems, only answers, you read the truth and follow the book, I've seen it all before you're not unique, this is all standard practice, it is all machine wrote and I will go through the stages, you will be cleansed down to the bone you will be broken and remoulded to the norm, don't take it personally, you're troubles now are ended I have come to save you, we all have to love the truth…begin the shots'

'Yes Drak I well know you're happy task, Vero a Mindfinder General and I will co-operate, but you must affirm the crime, I certain sure steer through the records of legend and lies as straight as a die, as a rook flies, without a deviation always following the trubook to the letter, I have deleted twelve percent of records in my pastime we are such stuff as rules are made on, and the faculty of histology is a beacon to the truth, there may be some mistake by some minion in my archivity and I will take the stroke but it is very small dross and not demanding level seven, five, eight assuredly, I do take it personally for myself it is psychotic soft and I feel the hurt in mind and body with pain unmeeted. Let the records speak, I am the judge and justify and purify the time gone by, I weep for Analog whence comes the crime?, I cry to Lordus where's the justice?'.

'Justice is an 'A' list word, justice like truth is in my hands, after your treatment you will know the justice and welcome its calm, your mind will be at peace. Now I will tell you of your crime, you see the party know that within our machines are a few, we think three 'black' machines full of antitruth designed for the contagion of this dread lie bacillus, to spread it through our peaceful world, destroying certainty, and that the disease is propagated through single units of the farting flexible, 'A' list community, they fart out heresy tied with a nosegay of fragrant culture, lies are exciting, truth is not and arsoles covet lies

We have the name or phrase 'Killagen', it is repeated again and again through your tribe, who is Killagen? He is quoted all the time, he is big and talks a lot in riddles, tell us his meaning and his place among you and you'll be free.

He is our leader, you will find him everywhere…….. Killagen was here.

He was here?, how could he be here, this is a party place and hidden from the world, no one exists in here, not Killagen, not you, you speak a fool.

Killagen is our lord and saviour and is every where, I brought him in with me

Killagen is not here and can't save you, you are unsaveable, you are ill and must be cured. We will kill Killagen.

So since we know wherein the illness lies we are systematically breaking you all out of existence. The cure for the plague is in the breaking, you're all guilty and must pay, and that's the truth.'

('give him the painshot to commence the pay.')

'I am a devout coward and will confess to any crime, the pain gives no result, I will tell you what you want to know. Just tell me of mine crime and I'll consent, there's no need to break me on the wheel or rack my mind, my mind's acceptance of your evidence will be complete. true I'm pure innocent, readout my pastimes there's no evidence, where's the proof?'.

The universal truth company knows all, we are the readers of your mind.

Before you came to kort you were convicted, all your clan has the plague, you must prove your purity. The resistance to logic brands you as a heretic, resistance is useless. Your default mode is in Histology, realise 402279H, the past is where the dead live with the lunatics and failures and doubt, we deal in surety and success. I am in the delete squad and if you bend you break, there's only one path to Lordus and your decadent tribe must walk it, before we mend, we break. I have total power and you have total hopelessness you're innocence only proves your guilt, admit it and stop all the pain to come for though I don't know the past I can foretell you're future. I give you one last chance to repent, and to aid you're decision, here is the wonder of our katekismantra which says it all and you know it.

In the pub the upper room was silent and focussed, the audience knew their stories and this was cool and impressively acted, he was either a superb teller, or mad, or both, even the bartender sat down, nobody interrupted though the permitted time span had long ago passed.

Drak cleared his throat, sipped his wine, lifted his glass as if to give a toast to the crowd, he closed his eyes and smiled and continued, "You have no idea of the intoxication of absolute power, the exhilaration of benign decisions for the common good, as you can see together with the coupling of painshots the option of recantation was offered, for above all we care. I hand to you a copy of our katekismantra which is the bedrock of our party, read it and understand our compassion for it is the truth.

You will see we have verified the language.

T TEI I IU LS

KATEKISMAI I IT IA

T IUT IS JUST
T IUT IS ST IEI IGT
T IUT IS LYT
LO IDUS IS T IUT
T IUT IS IYT
T IUT IS POWA
T IUT IS BU T E
A IT IS T IUT
I ELT IUT IS GUD
FALST IUT IS BAD
WE A I T ALFA AI ID T OMEGA
T IUT IS HA ID
WE A I T T IUT

'Truly the poetry of the truth, designed by Lordus the Great Mother on the first day of our party, pointing our path to realisation. You animals thrash about in your undesigned passion for you know not what, and gradually desire yourselves to death, you're units of despair, I salute you for your madness, another glass please.'

'I waited his reply which I knew would be denial, for how could he admit to the unknowable?, he was scheduled for reality. The goongards unshackled him from the chair, the kortgard was summoned and we processed to the reality room.

The reality room was large and made of silvery grey metal, running across the ceiling were metallic track ways from which were suspended lengths of cable and chains, placed around the walls were consoles studded with screens and pushbuttons and on the floor at intervals were circular, studded metal plates, It was like a precision engineering metal medical workshop it was a gleaming grey chamber and promised a sterile abattoir. There was the usual four technicians all dressed in black, masked with black hoods, we never hood the guilty, they must fear it all. The standard procedure for the breakdown is as follows; The deviant is stripped, then shackled at hands and feet, he has catheter shots in spine, heart and belly, and then the freedom cage is fitted, all this was done without problems'

'*I returned the Katekismantra with my reply that I admitted everything and anything, I was truly, truly guilty and truly sorry, my confession would be total.*

Drak said a deathbed confession was worthless and in vain, that I had been selected as guilty and his pleasure would be mine breakdown. With the gards I was marched to the reality room, the female chanting "Walk the way to the light, walk the walk"

And talk the talk methought, the walrus leads the way, this way to foolsworld

She was a true daughter of Lordus and intoned relevant clips from the book of rules, books which I myself had excavated from the past "I will lead you to the way, the truth and the light. The time has come, your time has come, this is the rightime." What's left I thought, what's left? I am the southpaw of research and deal in time, this is my bad time, they will edit me out of time my past will be modified.

The reality room was large and designed for fear with shackles from the roof and strange metal plates on the floor, there were four attendants in black overalls, black gloves, black hoods with eye slits covered with the ubiquitus black shades, nary one spoke, silent operators they knew the way to find the crime. Their whole device was one of remorseless stripping of the soul, no Analog would be left, I was distressed and shamed to be no more.

And to start the shaming they attacked the body, two operators grabbed mine arms and two with violence ripped off my garb the stripping of the soul starts with the stripping of the body, I was handcuffed and footcuffed, it was quickly and brutally done, I was naked and vulnerable and although it was warm, I shivered. I was still being held by the arms, one of the shackles was lowered from the roof, the end was soft and pliable it turned out to be a body harness which was strapped on from the neck to the crutch, Parts of the walls and equipment were polished metal, like a mirror and I could see myself in multi quavering images highlighting my ridicule and horror, verily a scene from hell. Nobody spoke, the only sound was my gibbering, giggling terror, I had been through Judgement Day and was one of the damned declining down to hell, it got worse, the female spoke an obvious ritual doggerel;

> *"Lordus, Great Mother lead him to the right*
> *Cast out the devils from his mindless plight*
> *We pledge to rid the party of a living lie*
> *Bring forth the cleansing of the freedom cage"*

The freedom cage came down, it was a small bell shaped cage of metal bars, it was put over mine head and fastened to the body harness and over that was placed a glass bubble, I looked like a naked spaceman, I began to smile at the quivering image in the walls for the look of me was laughable, I was a clown, mirror, mirror, on the wall who's the foolist of them all. The female stepped towards me she was holding a large plastic pistol, she shot me in the spine, the heart and then the belly, I thought the pain forehand was bad, this was unbearable, the fear and the pain forced me to my knees I was bleeding, this was the catheter gun that attached lines to my body for the stage to come, all this was done swiftly and silently, cold preparation for the interrorgation.

I was hoisted in the air, a metal plate moved on the floor to reveal a round black hole and I was plunged down, down into it, this was the reality chamber and was full of liquid. The lid clanged shut again and I was suspended in a black silent void

There was a click and the blinding light was in the chamber and never went off again and I was breathing through the freedom cage, the liquid supported me, I was floating, allowing me to focus on the throbbing pains.

The interrorgation began, I was in a tube one donc in diameter, on the curved wall postergraphs were playing showing trudiscs of our world and of Lordus. Sound was input through phones in the freedom cage, there was a soft click as they were switched on and soft musik began to play, slow wonderful Mozart filled my head. Then the female spoke in a slow flat expressionless voice

'You face this court under the indictment FALSETRUTH and will answer the questions put to you.

The interrogation is not for us to find the truth, we know the truth.

The questions are merely the method for you to find reality.

The voice had a downward inflexion at the end of each statement, she sounded depressed.

Since we already know the answers each lie prolongs the interview.

'The door is locked.

Only one answer is permissible, only one answer is correct.

Incorrect thoughts must be rectified

She paused frequently but the music was beautifully continuous, framing each question, I didn't interrupt, I just listened.

Discomfort is part of the learning process

Remember, your normality is our aim

The party knows your past, present and future.

The monologue continued.

The door is locked.

We are a caring court and we are the way, the truth and the right.

Truth is warm, truth is pure, truth is the way.

This is the time, your time, prepare yourself.

There was a click the music stopped, the only sound was my laboured breathing in the cage...........I wept for Analog

Truthkort seven, five, eight in session this is a continuous investigation until you know the truth, answer the questions as required. The investigation will be conducted by Truthmaster Drak, the investigation begins.......

There was static for a minute then a click, again music was playing but this time wild, strident, disjointed, foreign. Then the voice spoke it was masculine, quiet, almost a whisper but harsh and guttural.

State your name and number'

Heartsatease Analog, Number A96402279H

State your age and address

Seven nine yarns old, my block is Veracity Tower four, two, three, three, six, Unit eight

In employment, would you say your work was correct?.

At last I thought, the chance to show my worth and voice a protest, I am a model of corre............

Have you a correct relationship with your underlings?, we need to find your mind, where are you Analog?.

..........ct procedure, a timemaster of,.......the dronevoice continued without pause and I realised he wasn't listening, it was a standard pre-recorded farce, I was talking to myself on a talktimeloop The pain was hurting inside,

Do you love your partner?

Do you love the Lordus?

Do you love the party

The door is locked.

Enough! Turn off the pain, I am guilty, turn it off I confess. Tell me of my crimes

The pains improve me, verily I remember all now and will speak true.

We wish to know of other deviants, will you give us names and numbers

We know you are in cells of three, trios you call trinity's

Do you follow the true way in everything?.

The door is locked

The pain in the spine was invading the whole body, I was sick and pleaded for the end of it, I was becoming pain, nothing else existed in my world.

As you know in all things there is but one way

In work there is but one way

In food there is but one way

In musik there is but one way

in sex there is but one way

In life there is but one way..............the true way.

The door is locked

Recognise that your fantasies, delusions, dreams are known and noted and deleted, you come to the way in the end. Don't you realise that a million dregs have been broken on the reality rack, there is only one way out, we go on forever, forever, forever more, time has ceased to exist.

Drak was animated now, he had removed his jacket and had progressed on to a bottle of wine, the room was very warm and in the spotlight he was warmer still, he was leaning forward on his chair focussing on the story and the crowd, speaking louder, it was becoming ridiculously serious. the club was silent and was taking it seriously.

'I wonder if you realise how primitive you are?, this backtime experience for me is sordid, and the effort to downplot the problem to your level is hard, I'm not sure you will grasp the danger or can help, but I am desperate. We have used one yarn to try and crack the code without readout and my moment of decision has begun.'.

'He was hoisted in the air, a cover was removed from a reality chamber and he was dropped into the pod and we started processing, its all standard and automatic, he was filleted with open ended, endless questions, with constant repetitive images, with bright light all the time, and through the catheters the application of pain and medical stimuli. It goes on for ever, or until they break then we remove the fault and fill with reality, I have done it In many pastimes it is the pain that brings release, once they are focussed the end comes The A list are the longest, but on the third day he broke.'

The...door is....looked

Why persist with…delusions, you will come to…the way in the end

I couldn't retch any more there was nothing inside any more. I was just a carcase of pain, decomposing into the liquid, I had ceased to exist. And then I spoke the truth, 'This is the heart of Heartsatease, I unlock the thoughts and show you the fabric, the fabrication of the machines that read and regiment our souls'. Cry for the souls downgrade in Veracity, cry for civilisation reduced to party truth, weep for the pity of it all. Lordus doesn't exist, she's an image, an imagination, Does the party exist? do you exist?, cut yourself, let me see blood, let me smell the blood.

I need a proof resistable not a readout, this is the truth I believe in me alone.'

still the voice went on.

I will break you to the bone, you will only believe in pain, the pain is proof positive you exist, then you will believe in me the pain giver. The power of pain is irresistible, your whole being will concentrate on it.

Then justice, love, jealousy, duty will be no more and you will be no more, you will be empty until we fill you up.

I go on forever, the party goes on forever…..we see all, we know all……there is only one way out

The doors locked………….

'I rotated in the liquid air and hung upwards in my chains, down is up, the world was all together different now, I viewed my feet floating above my head with interest.

How sweet the sound the silence makes knocking at the locked door, knock. knock down the door to freedoms cage to set me loose to sing the song of freedom, for I'm the jester at the kort when folly reigns and madness walks the chambers of the night, I know the dead and will wake them to circle in the dance of death, I am living yet am dead, a husk, a chrysalis to metamorphosis into newtruth the hydra truth with many arms embracing the dawn of a destiny where Lordus is my handmaiden and all things including madness are considered.

I've gotta motta, always's merry and bright,

look around you will fined

every cloud is silver lined.

The sun will shine although the sky's a grey one,

I've pften said to meself I've said

cheer up cully you'll soon be dead

a short life and a gay one.

A short life and a grey one

The new prawn shines on the setting of Lordus light going down, down the dark road from the north came the monster Shattermouth, I am come death the eater of worlds, lament for the going down of the light, a lachrymose lament for designs downfall and the rising of living and lies and freedom to be free, how sweet the sound of silence.

Oh lament for poor Heartsatease!

For he is broken on the wheel and it has broke my heart.

He was a doughty blade and slew the many dragons in the tale. His sword of truth was mighty in the book.

He had crossed the river of reality, he had passed the past and the black gard dog, he had crossed the desert of despair, he had laid waste the unterwerk, a peradventure for the Lordus to delight.

My pain has ended and I float down, up the tube and view the downworld posters as they float by, there is only one way and that is down, and that's the truth
>*float by*   *and that is down*
>>*down the dark road*
>>*downfall down*
>*The new up is down*
>*The truth is down the tube, a peradventure*
What is the magic country that lies after down?.
>*I wish I was down, down the*

I twirled and rotated in my tube of death, my focus was more and more on a huge image of the Lordus face speaking to me alone through the ever changing ring of the luscious lips, the succulent vaginal voice …. and my feet. And then I spied a shape rising to hide mine feet,… it was half down my body…, it was my longmost dormant dikon,…. King Richard the new lord of all, the life giver, it grew and grew prodigious quick until it was as large as me and it was in control a giant in the tube, it ruled the tube,……. it was more alive than me, I was an appendage. I rotated in the tube The Lordus face mouthed the universal truths out of a large pouting 'O' of a black lipped mouth, the Richard ranged round, an animal seeking freedom it looked at the lips, it didn't like it, it was offended, it reared and then it struck straight into the many shaped thick ring of the mouth of truth…. Lordus was full shocked, her eyes widened and her cheeks inflated, she was angerful, and then she did the most ferocious, terrible, reaction, a clanging trap of pain, the frown turned to smile, the smile widened into a grimace showing all the teeth and then the mouth was opened wider still, and then she bit with all her might.'

'On the third day we heard the scream through the cover and we new he was finished.'……

Drak was pacing along the edge of the stage like a caged animal and gesticulating wildly., he was just in control, he frothed and roared to good effect if this was acting it was primal, or he was mad.

'Upon my signal the cover was opened and Analog raised, he burst forth onto the staging, a cascading liquid shape flowing with multi coloured fluids, he hung there in his chains. We have never lost a deviant in our enquiries, no one ever dies, upon my signal the female stepped forwards with the gun to give as usual, the resurrection shot into the heart portal. But then she stopped, and this is how he won victorious, for there was no portal there, as he was rising from the pod he must have used the bracelets to rip it out, all there was, was a large uneven bleeding hole dribbling life onto the floor,

The female lost her reason, she cut the cables holding him aloft and he crashed onto the floor, smashing the freedom cage he lay on his back smiling at the lights above, she then without reason tried to administer the shot into the gaping hole this was not a reeltruth reaction. As she knelt by his side, he was lying on his back with open, staring, unseeing eyes, his mouth bubbling froth with a slight rictus smile, and then he spoke to her the few words that we need to know. Her reply was to stand up, throw down the gun, kick him in the side, and then step on his neck, rupturing his windpipe and the brain stem dock'.

There was now reaction in the audience about the strength of the material, the story had gone too far, and the acting too real. But Drak would not be denied, he leant out, cantilevered out from the edge of the stage, he was holding a piece of crumpled paper in his hand, he brandished it aloft. 'This is the reason I am here, I need the truth, hear me out', the compare pacified the scene for the tale was very near the end and Drax continued in a noisy room.

We had a complete record of the crime and forensically examined every second of the case, all had been run to the trubook except the resurrection mode where madness had prevailed. We knew he was leader of a trio, the series of interlinked cells that honeycomb the 'A' fraternity the poison troops that spread the madness in their ranks. His death proved his vice, but though his death had been his victory, it left us problems we have to be solve, which were the action of the female, and the riddle of his message to her., if we can solve them we have a breakthrough. The female we realise was part of the cell, we have examined her down to zero but she shows nothing and her body is now stored in a retrieval pod. Her actions have two solutions, of course only one of which is true. She either felt pity for him and put him out of pain, a ridiculous, untrue solution for pity and sorrow are delusions, or she was part of his triangle and had to delete him before he spoke again, he had to be silenced.

Drak paused and unrolled the paper in his sweaty palm, he held it in both hands aloft and showed it to the room. 'These are the last words he spoke, digitally retrieved from the freedom cage, they are mysterious and mean nothing and therefore logically must be in code. We have spent one yarn to break the code, we broke the female but not this. Now comes the reason I am here'. His speech was now more urgent, more rapid, he was gabbling he was obviously mad. 'Another reason for the woman's act was anger, she knew his death proclaimed the end of her, no one dies in our protection, and after her the quest goes on, we never give up. We now examine the next one up the chain, which is me and I will break. I have come back because I know nothing and that's the truth, but in finding that I am pure we will destroy me, I am expendable and will end up as nothing in a pod.

To think that I, Drak, defender of the truth, reality's champion, the unwavering, unbending, zealot of the way should cease to exist is unbearable, is so unjust. And so I come back to a simpler world to find the answer in your cruder minds or else I stay here till I die, for Analog lived in the past and that's where the truth lies. His riddle leads to the triumvirate, the trinity, the trio, his speech is short but is the first crack in their way and if we break one, we break all. But also after my tragic end the machines go on up the pyramid triangulating outwards till they find the triple traitor …..who isn't there, deleting the truth as they go we never give up, I need the answer or I live no more either in this world or the other, the lead is very slender, just a few words let slip as he was broke, but you can set us free to perfect our perfect world, our Vera-city. Here are the lying nonsense words we have to break, we need to know the truth.

He said……

The bitch has stamped the life from me, and I lie melting on the floor, I will lie myself to death and soak myself in truth. For I have found the truth in the party, the truth of Lordus in the web, a surety I will crack her. I will crack her like I smash the buk

The dog has out bitedout the throat and spat on the floor my voice… is gone………..I speak in doggerel

Now ends the song of Analog………Lordus dies with me The priest of glory…………… blest trinity………

Where lies the blest best three, pick the card, find the lady.

My midsummer nightmare now has ended……….Amazing race…

(the voice was soft and husky, almost a gargle)

I will smash her into smithereens, into stardust

Lucid Lucy in the sky with stars, Apollo rides the sky, the son shining in the sky

how sweet the sound that silence makes knocking at the door……….

My dream is done, three at last …He said ….Three at last, three at last, three at last, thank god almighty, three at last.

Credo

You think I came to talk you beauty,
the saccharine, sentimental seduction
Of the harlots tongue.
That everything will be sunshine and light,
with loveliness, balance and everything right
and all that crap.
You think I come to write you surety,
I write not what you want to hear
but what is true.
The theme is nature red, yellow, blue, raw
in carnivorous tooth and slavering claw.
The theme is life.
Kafka, Goya, Bosch, they lead the way.
Life is black with pools of light
for fools to bathe in.
Our journey is through uncaring country
where you are just a number to be
Erased.

About the ending and everything sad,
about satisfying revenge and cruelty
And eviscerating failure.
Dream your sad life away my friend
you will come to the truth in the end,
there's no escape.
You are not here to enjoy,
but to suffer,
I hurt therefore I am.
You are not here to understand
but to feel and
calibrate the pain.

But then again, I lie a lot

Cavalcade

The light was different from all the others,
a dark star in the night
Brooding and pulsating ahead of them
a fixed point in the west
towards the setting of the sun.
It was a quiet, dusty cavalcade
chinking through the night
There was no beaten path to follow,
only the fixed star lighting the way.
The journey had been long
and they were old and weary,
so they talked as they rode
As the prophet told it long ago
and the oracle today
So it was spoken and written in the stars
About the babe of salvation and sorrow
about the omen in the sky.
What was its portent to them all
was it good news for the world,
the birth of a new life on the road
to the meaning of it all.
So that being lost would end
and they would find their way
by this signpost in the sky,
Surely, surely, surely they followed it.
They followed it with hope
for the light was significant,
unlike in history anything before,
it meant either the saving of the world
Or its death
For it was a dark star.

Conversation

She came upon the bus spitting fire
Her companion trailing in her wake
And asked the driver loudly
"dose this go to chapel hill?"
The driver nodded quietly
He knew an affirmative was needed
Even if he had to leave his route.
She flashed her pass dramatically
And stomped down to the back
of the bus, dramatically
Her mate followed resignedly
They were both Asian teenagers
Dressed in black with hoods up
For it was raining bad
"That fucking wanker, I'll get him",
She spoke loudly, all the bus
could hear and flinched.
"He told me he was in
And she was fucking nothing,
I'll get the fucking bastard".
She paused for breath,
Her command of anglo-saxon was spot-on impressive
Her mate mumbled something,
"whats that arseole done?,
I tell you what he's done
He's broke my fucking heart,   that's all."
The bus was filling up
and was listening with open mouths
The older women winced, were deaf
and clenched their teeth and sighed
"I'll never see that prick again
But when I fucking do........."
Her mobile rang, it was the boy
"fuck you mate, you're shit
I'll get you, yes I will'
I don't want no fucking excuses,
You dickead
I remember forever you fucking shit
You and her are fucking dead."
She paused for breath and effect,
he obviously spoke probably softly.
"Oh....... piss off you twat"

She got up and walked down the bus,
she'd missed her stop.
and glared at the driver, a man,
She waited for the doors to open
impatiently with fists clenched,
wanting to punch someone,
hoping to be irritated . . .
They got off and walked back
in the drizzling rain still talking.
She had been wonderfully, powerfully,
incandescently frightening,
She was the stuff of legend
She was Medea, Lady Macbeth
And the Wife of Bath
All rolled into one
Such teenage passion!
She had set down a mark
The boy would be thrilled,
she was thrilled
and the bus was thrilled
And the making up would be good
The bus dawdled on down the road,
relaxed and went to sleep.

Clink

The prison is very large
And you have spent your life
designing and constructing it.
Cell by cell, stone by stone,
lock by lock, and chained to the wall is you.
You eat your daily bread
You contemplate the grinding boredom of it all
and of the job monotonous,
with partner incredulous
Children disappointing and detached,
in housing disappointing and detached
and costly
in the wrong place.
Its bearable as long as you don't think
which after a few years
is easy enough to do.
The trick is to concentrate on nothing
with all your might
one day at a time
It's the only way to beat a life sentence,
to become detached yourself
and deceive yourself, so that you live in a lie
of your own construction.
We are such stuff as lies are made of,
and our little life is rounded in deceit.
It's the only thing that keeps us going.
END GAME
I knew it was coming long time,
like a train smash down the line
hitting the brick wall and stopping dead.
The pain it is increasing and focuses my mind,
not on the pain, but my endeavours
To create pieces of me in art
So it has its virtues.
Sometimes the pain frustrates my move,
and I am impotent in my desire
and rage against infirmity
For I have the money to be comfortable
and pain free with a pill
and exist in chair bound futility

To exist but not to live.
We are born with hurt and live with it,
the background noise in every breath.
And now I equate pain with living,
and believe painless to be dead
and so I say that at my end game
in the crash the pain will cease,
And all of you will die.

Examples

There's nothing sadder than the ice cream cone
dropped on the road, the irredeemable anguish of loss.
The drunk in the gutter has the soundest sleep,
immune from fear and pain In comfy - cosy lunacy
and snoring with an easy mind.
Nothings older than the failure seen
and bitterest is what might have been
when dreams are dashed in life's reality.
And youngest is the spring, new and green
thrusting for the light and the promise of the day.
The softest is a boy in love
with sighing, yearning delusions on the focussed one.
Nothing harder than a woman's scorn
with cruellist words oiled by the bile of hurt
Cascading forth.
None so corrupt as politico's, because they start so high
with ideals fit to change the world, before the cankerous worm sets in the apple - expedient.
The grossest concept realised - the fart in church.
Most troubled is the artist
struggling for truth inside himself
when all the world wants lies.
Most beauty is the cub, the foal, the babe
in proportion, grace and innocence perfect.
The greatest pain is love,
the greatest gift is love

Jean

My sister Jean came ten years after me
A much desired delicate perfect bundle
To brighten up a bad war for the family
To grow up beautiful and strong
To be the apple of her fathers eye
To be the carbon copy of her mom
To be the bond and support of my brother
And to be the joy of everyday to me.
All our talents copied in her DNA,
but all our flaws deleted
So that by sense and gentleness
straightening out us sibling clods
So that life had meaning, above all happiness
by her example.
The linchpin in our family uniting us
against our urge to self destruct.
The one sure northern star in our firmament
how we relied on you
.The blessing and the answer to our world
In our wasted world
But on the seventh month she went away,
she never made it to the light
and never saw the sun or me,
and left us on our own.

Myosotis

If only I could win the game, just once
and be victorious in the battle.
I am a member of the great unsung,
and know my purpose in the scheme.
I am, like everyone and everyman,
the unknown and the known,
The unwashed peasant in the wilderness,
The prince of plenty in the pleasure dome,
The iron criminal in the underworld,
The wild madman in the frightening cell,
The celebrity and star in wonderland
are all forgotten by the next years throng.
For I am in the jostling throng
and only there to make the numbers up
Gods plaything in the game of life
to amuse the master with my strategy.

I plan my gambits in the play
and strive to famously succeed.
My moves are meaningful, subtle,
intelligent and focussed
and laughable.
And I kid myself that it's
not the winning, but the taking part,
not for winning but failing desperately.
But I know in the end,
at the death, I loose the game.
Be you so rich and famous on the day
you are with me always
in the 'f' word gang.
Forgotten.

Midsummer Night

I come to you from fairyland
And I am hard, and I am strong,
And nameless is my name.
Before the cross, before the oak and ash
I was.
Dreamcatcher of your sleeping soul,
I spin the thoughts of gossamer
That bind you in your beds
As I knew you in the womb so I live inside you,
your nightime parasite.
Your terror incognito
Beyond the trees I set my snare
For darkness is my trap,
And nightmare is my song.
Beware me, I am the scream in the night.

Moonlight

Light was the night, the sky lustrous warm.
The moon sprayed the earth with silver, liquefying the ground.
And on the hills the sheep stood silent, waiting.
The fox and badger ceased their prowl to watch
and owls were stone stock still among the trees,
the leaves whispered,
quieted by the procession through the dell
Jack-o-lanterns starred the slopes
to mirror the low slung heaven
so that the sky shone with stardust close enough to touch.
The earth was breathing, and the air was warm as blood
Soft as silk, the breeze breathed magic through the dell
and all the world stood tiptoe on this night.
The promenade came dancing, skipping through the wood
for this was the night
The music was light, small and wonderful
and they danced to the rhythm of the night
They lit the way with torches, whirling, swirling as they went
a spluttering gleaming line of fire,
and carried garlands, bowls, baskets
as offerings to the power in the night.
A cavalcade of joy, a ribbon of delight.
They surfed through long grass in the meadow
and shepherds on the hills called forth their dogs
to join the throng.
And they all sang the song.
For what is ritual without the song and dance?
And what is ceremony without music?
They praised the sky, they praised the moon
and the garden of delights.
They exalted in the universe.
and walked towards the sacred grove deep in the wood
chanting as they went the age old rhymes
that they were alive in such a time
and felt the glory in the moonlit air.
To witness perfection before the dawn,
the time had come to praise the wood
and signify its power complete.
Before the dawn would come.

My Hate Song

I know that hating isn't good
because it hurts yourself,
So I don't.
But if I did there's only one I'd hate
And vent my rage on
with all my fury,

I am a dreamer, and I dream a lot,
and sometimes when I'm feeling low
I dream revenge,
I fantasise on how he'll get his due
and dream how he would suffer and
rot in hell.

He's hard to describe without being obscene
For calling him an affluent arrogant
arsehole
Would scarcely be accurate
and is lost in translation.
Because he's not.

His complete complacent indifference
means he's forgotten my name
and my hurt.
Anger is self destructive, and so
I leave him to destroy me
in his own good time.

And so I know that hating is bad.
But if I did,
it would be him I'd loath.
and I would fall in hate with him
and compose a hate song.
Which this is.

Pissartist

Post prandial parson, position prone
in private pew phucks powerfully
the pliable promiscuous passion person
prostitute 'Pearl'.
Picture the pornographic pair,
the pious and profane,
in profuse perspiring pants.
pursuing primogeniture.

Pre-time, prelates prima partner, pragmatic, psychotic 'Pauline'
posits poison potion per palatable pancake
'pon the preacher's pudding plate.
Passion prompts purple pontiff's pelvic pyrotechnic push onto plush pudenda place.
Pleasure past, poison prompts post mortem,
push alas a parting shot.
Paradise lost, parachutes out life's plane
to pyro-Pandemonium.

Poet peasant poacher prowls the pasture,
pockets packed and pistol primed.
Passes preaching porch pastoral,
peeps panic pitter patter Pearl.
Pink person plops persuasively
in puddled paddock path and
ply's her plea for problems pardon,
perhaps to pack away the priest?.
Playmate pose provocative to
promise payment profuse and prompt.
Powerful pagan potato ploughman
pats and paddles pliant person,
persuaded to plunder posthumous padre
and place in pesthole privately.
Promised pots of pleasure with pneumatic pulchritude.

Passionate peasant picksup parson
plops into the private place.
Pronto pierced by prongs of pitchfork
pushed by perfumed phenomenon,
Purple puss pours from pustules
in the prostrate prole's prostate

Peasant and preacher packed peaceful,
Potted and paired for posterity.
Pronto, pads away priceless Pearl.
Now, pantomime is played,

PHINIS

PROVERB, Private pleasures promote peril

Reverie

Write me a riot
so that I feel alive
in the tedium of today
and laze in ersatz violence
safe in second hand sounds
and thrill to the gabble of life.

My life is dreadful dull
and needs a shot of liberation
to dramatize existence
I feel the need to feel
be it pity, sadness, rage, exultation
or a kick up the backside.

Read me a poem
of the revolution yet to come
where death walks the land
and nothing is left
on the face of the earth or under
except my mind and me.

Or perhaps a play
of lacerating love that fills the air
with wonder and romance
and flowers and blossom
and food and wine perfume my mind
with sweet sumptuous desire

I am in need of a breeze
to send me from the doldrums
to float my boat to new worlds
unimagined and undreamt
where I can live and live again
a dream a day until I die.

Righteeous Rhyme

You ain't got no right to freedom,
you aint got no right to joy
Not food, nor comfort, riches
not nothing, honest boy.
Living is a toilsome trouble
wherein there's gains and loss
You play the game for real
governed by the dices toss.
Its six to one you loose it,
the dealer loads the force
and you don't even have the right
to spit upon the course.
The battle's never ending
For the poor, the weak, the lame
they are the silent people
With no rights, no voice, no name.
Long or short the trial is weighted
against the rights of man,
fortune favours nothing
in your littlesome lifespan.
The fight is for the high ground
above the milling throng,
the high pleasure meadows
where the treasures for the strong
You aint with the righteous
you're the wrong side of the tracks
For the money buys the good times
climbing on the peoples backs
You have the right to hunger,
you have the right to pain,
the right to keening sorrow
standing silent in the rain.
They say we're something special,
but we fool ourselves and lie,
you got the right for breathing,
'til you reach the right to die.

Sea Shanty

In Valparaiso lived a witch,
languorous and long
seductive deadly was the bitch
Sirenic was her song.
She was the purest, finest, baddest
Gladdest in the row,
Glorious in the ruin game
thrallsome in the throw
Lads mark well what I do sing
And dance the jig and hornpipe
To the high step of the devil fling
Heel and toe me hearties
She sang her echo song from caverns
High above the strand
Shiver silver was the sea,
Golden was the sand
She called to lovesick men of love,
She played the theme of lust
They heard the melody and wept
saw beauty in the rust.
Lads mark well what I do sing
And dance the jig and hornpipe
To the high step of the devil fling
Heel and toe me hearties
The warlocks served her well
And satisfied her need
To bind the victims in her web
To sleep in soft scaled reed
Familiar was her snake,
Dancing in its skin
Servile to her every word
A jewelled rope of sin
Lads mark well what I do sing
And dance the jig and hornpipe
To the high step of the devil fling
Heel and toe me hearties
They sleep their life away
In desire's content
Of dewdrop drugged impotence
Sorrowful and silent

Delirious in her infamy
Drowsy in their chains
Indolent in misery
A slavery of pains
Lads mark well what I do sing
And dance the jig and hornpipe
To the high step of the devil fling
Heel and toe me hearties

Shaman

Necromancy praxelut,
breaker nocturnaly.
Crux eternal blud and red.
Lupus, ursine, carnivory.
The raven talks, the song is told
Glory for the chosen.
Lite the torch inside the hall,
kall the hounds to mustre.
Blakis blakis blakis the cross,
blanche the bone viscerus.
Sullen, sad and saturnine
kum to us disnachte.
Allustre to the alterstroke,
Allmeryt to the masterstroke.
Klenz the sin of man in blud,
Mortus, mortus, mortus
end the line.

Storytime

The news was bad again today.
The screen was showing bits of fire and lots of smoke
and bits of people screaming, mouths agape
and hands aloft with fingers spread.
They shouted at me through the fog,
I turned the sound off.
I had to get a cloth with disinfectant on
and wipe the screen clean
of all the blood and gore,
but I couldn't loose the smell.

I eat my meal from a tray on my lap
while they explained how we were winning,
this was the final push.
And all our killings were justified
or a tragic mistake.
Everything explained that we were never wrong,
that we were fighting for the right to rule the world.
That we would save the world - for us,
and peace was safe in our hands,
but I had blood upon my hands.
Freedoms blood.

At the end they showed us sport
and how we had lost unluckily,
but our triumph of a bronze in something vague.
The weather report was severe,
the danger of one inch of snow
so people shouldn't venture out.
The good news was a moisturizer
and a friendly car,
for we are worth it.
And tomorrow is another day.

Table Talk

Through the open window
comes the sound
of the outside coming in.,
The drone of life
and the faint song of a bird singing
The quietness of the milk
bottle on the table,
half full and white as silk
on Snow White's neck.
Part exhausted in the morning light.
the surface slightly quivers
Unreasonably,
for no vibrations sense the air
or the tables gravitas.
It's played its part in the breakfast show
morphing the cereal and the tea
to fondfood light and sweet.
The shape and blue cap
a symbolic icon of fertility,
part of the silent still life composition.
The weighty tea pot smoulders,
steaming for the second cup
and bides its time to pour
the scalding power.
The confined engine of burning desire.
Rotund and hermaphrodite,
male and female in a smooth
and single shape
Longing for action.
through the pouting, steaming spout.
And the table stands foursquare
supporting this still, stillest life
with comfortable ease
serene in its confidence
and the memory of long days past in the sun.
And with the certainty
of lunch and dinner yet to come,
with different shapes and smells
occupying the top with pleasure.
And the treasure of table talk forever more.

Tango

The talk is soft and gentle in the soft dark linen tent,
the talk of loving nonsense in the silence of the room
They are content.
And tender is the touch of recognition
in the pleasure
and delightful pain to come.

The exploration of the lands and continents,
whisper talk becomes instructions and demands.
The sweet sweat out the partial pores,
shiver wave that brings delight explodes the mind.
Now sweating squirming pressure pleasure

The tousled sheets are tangled with the bodies
in the actions spin, hot is the bundle.
And frantic the focus on the senses.
in luscious triple tingle gasping for air
gyrating, fighting for the ultimate.

Atop, the titivating, titillating mountains feel the way
to mount the pouting mounts.
Corruptions in the loins rampant
and the prick, prick, prickling of the plough.
The 'V' line is the flight path
to the undiscovered open countryside.

And the connection is made, they interlock.
The continents combine
in one flexible malleable, terrible animal,
beached and open mouthed
words loose their meaning, mindless is the animal.
And sensation fills the world.

Stonethefu..........stonethefu
Stonethefu.........stonethefu
Stonethefu.........stonethefu
Stonethefugh..........stonethefugh…............stonethefugh

KERISTE!.

The Dancer

She came at eve to dance with me.
A close together waltz,
she floated syncopating to the song in perfect time.
A perfect partner in the dance
our steps became as one
and I was lost in ecstasy.
She called the tune to dance the night away
in whirling swirling rhythm,
the coaxing comfortable beat,
and we both knew the time,
It was my time.

She came to me in bed that night,
and whispered in my ear
and stroked my cheek.
I lay there sightless in the sheets,
stranded on the strand.
She covered me,
and fucked
and sucked my life away,
a consummation to be wished,
sweet it was to cease the pain in one big sigh.
It was my time.

The End

The high cross was highest on the hill.
The soldiers placed him at the top,
the military choice
dominating the area.
And from his vantage point he saw the world
across the lucent painful plain.

It was always best to have the high ground,
the imperials had seen it all before.
Foreigners in a foreign land watch their backs
The discipline and routine in their life
brought civilization to the world,
and their literature was written in red

But above them all, on the tree
he hung, stapled to the cross.
And like those with leisure at their death
he contemplated time,
he saw the past and knew his future
and marveled at the beauty of it all.

The city spread before them down the hill.
First of all the groups around the criminals
to see the circus play.
An ant hill, with ribbons of ants scurrying
to the meat, to see the drama unfold
and how they would die.

The central criminal was talking incessant,
talking to the pain.
The brain was concentrating on the pain,
the pain was universal and dominating,
it rolled over him in waves of grinding fire
quickening, in rhythm with his breathing and his pulse.

The soldiers were tired, tired of the people and the day,
the day had turned tedious
in its inevitable, predictable end.
They turned their backs on the cross and faced the city.
and wrapped their cloaks around them tight,
it was getting cold, a storm was coming.

The Gift

The sun has burst in the leaden sky
in shards and smithereens of light,
and a perfect burnished bow
is arced above the world.
All the ordered colours shiver delight
and bedazzle the stand alone in awe.
A kaleidoscope of silent song.
Who draws the bow that has no reason
and serves no purpose, only wonderment?.
A silent, fading glimpse of paradise,
a waxing, waning image that infantasizes all.
So we are silent, like the bow
and rejoin our primary days
in shining primary colours
A quiet shimmering statement of sublime
as fragile fragments of the universe.
Designed by nature, and given free,
as an overarching glittering gift.
The unique marvel of the firmament
And a cause for contemplation
that only we appreciate.
A pagan power that's indestructible
and everlasting in its sweet ephemera,
made for the child of every age.
Simple in art, but enigmatic bold
and in a whisper unfolds its grand design.
O memorable ghostly fleeting mirage!,
a glory made for us alone.

The Sentence

It feels good coiled up in the dark,
out of harms way and harmless
and safe and sound
The sounds are muffled through the wall
and sound reassuring.
so that contentment fills the space.
Drowsily I take my fill and feel the power
I am at peace and growing stronger by the hour
and soon will break my bonds.
The time was set to be free, a prisoner no longer.
A prisoner no longer,
Spring was coming to my cell
fed and watered by my guard.
Guardedly not knowing day from night,
Blind as hairless Samson in the tent
in the silent soft shelled cell,
compressed, strapped to the walls
a demanding servitude searching for the light,
a demanding ego in the pod.
not knowing that I exist
Not knowing that I exist,
in solitary confinement,
I do nothing, for I can do nothing
powerless in my pod planning
but feeling the hunger growing,
I stretch myself and test the walls
my strength will burst the shell
then the pain will set me free
out of the dark to the light
Into the green and throbbing day.
Into the green and throbbing day,
the throbbing in my head
matches the throbbing of the engine
in the next room
incessant and dominating my cell,
so that the walls pulsate in rhythm
to the beat in my head, head, head.
It is my strobeing universe
I long for the silence of freedom
after the big bang.

The Song

Sing the sleepy song of Summertime,
The melody of the scented,
apple dappled air,
the drowsy buzzing
of the bumblebees.
The luxuriatus of lying down
in high straw grass
of meadows of desire.
To drink the grape and apple
till you reel and fall upwards
to the warm blue sky.
You laugh till tears of joy
run down your cheeks
and mingle with the juice of freedom
from your lips.
The languid torpor

Sleep Time

I had a strange long dream last night,
Initially based in the shop,
on a busy hustling bustling satisfying day,
It was a daydream.
And later in a room with French windows
at a function with food, music
it was peopled with family and friends,
a party or celebration.
In the first part Charles was very unpleasant,
which was unusual.
And in the second the room was full and overflowed
through the windows.
It was a warm night and an enjoyable occasion,
the wine flowed
the dancing and the conversation flowed
I knew everyone.
It was late when I left and walked my way home
in the warm night air,
Thinking of the happy time, bemused and happy,
but on the way
I was downed and as I lay on the ground
I wrote in troubled blood
"I LOVE YOU ALL"……..how strange.

Humouresque

Tis nevermore I go to see it,
Tis never less I go away.
For all the world is in the seeing,
thinking's for another day.
Judge not the action badinage.
Where's the beef sweet Adeline?.
I'm happy as a cow in clover,
sodden in the Rhenish wine.
The clotted cream also rises,
at the dawning of the night
and the moonset's blue horizon
hides the drowning of the light.
Dirty rhymes and filthy stanzas
validate the second rate.
The chocolate chip of pies immortal
lie crumbled on the Hatter's plate.
Ah the triumph in the earhole,
The lap of honour pornograph
Sweet's the toffee apple broken
The joke is on the other laugh.
The puddle in the gutter glistens
with the fool's gold lightening flash.
The music of imagination
Is jazzed up in the cymbals crash
Culture floods us to our armpits.
We are saturation drowning
swim for the mudflats mediocre
the circus of moonface clowning.
Blessed are the blinded looters
hoovering up and mowing down
the jam mines bucket shopping,
the tragedy of Tinsel town
Crown me with the thorns of plenty.
puncture me with howls of glee,
The shoe is on the other tweedle
for on the treadmill is dum me

Sheltering

She sat in the corner of the bus shelter,
she was, to use an old word, a tramp.
With two sticks to lurch her way along
A dumpy tied together figure,
a loose strung parcel of neglect
hiding the underneath from view.
Her mac was grey and mottled black,
her hands were grey and shiny black,
her face was red and foggy black.
Her hair was scrawny frothy grey,
and round her chin she had
whispy long white hair that showed
the first flowering of a beard,
like old marooned Ben Gunn.
she needed cheese and cherishing.
She looked older than she was,
probably about sixty summers on the road.
She spoke with a certain delicacy
and looked through slit eyes at the world
as if wincing at the sight
and the blows to come.
And yet when they did open
they were cornflower blue
and shone from out a smoky face
an innocent child within the husk.
But there's no one to care
where she does eat and sleep,
she obviously doesn't wash.
And what's her given name?,
The only gift she's ever had.

The Flower

The flower has burst its shell like thunder,
from out the earth the green shell shoots
the world to its firedark centre.
The roots ignite the fire of life
ten thousand miles away the shot is heard,
and the globe shudders with the shock.
Its feet are standfast in the clay
Its head is questing for the sun
The dewdrop on the petal lakes
The head and makes a countryside.
The colours erupt like starbursts
in the grass green world of summer.
Seeking the light it climbs towards the sun
and will reach it by sundown.
The next day it will flare and flame
for one day, then wither on the vine
and hang its fragile crumbling head,
brown, and fall from grace
and fall to grass, straw on straw.
And rain its seed, soft as a butterfly
upon the wind and die a year away.

the soft explosive echo rocking

The Dead Line 2020

For twenty years we've fought the war
In the hot desert land
And the emerald city
And in the eastern promise.
We've buckled on the shield of justice
We've sharpened up the sword of woe
Marching to the beat of drum skins
In the song that never ends
In the long view we will triumph
over foes that will not fight
proper battles with some tactics
in the darkness of the night.
Long ago we knew the outcome
would be swift and recondite.
Now we die in wayside ditches,
they will shift and fade away
Our sons now are fighting wars
that we started long ago
for a cause we don't remember.
Like the sand, the deadlines shift,
They pray to god in strident voice
at end of day or week or year
They are waiting for their deadline
lined up and numbered in a row
Another decade, another peace
To fight for
Another target for the upper brass,
Another target for the guns
Another city left in rubble
Another century of loss
Another marker left to mark the spot,
Another body bag..............amen.

The View

She was in the pound shop,
a pretty brunette, smiling
with her ten year old son
One stop in front of me in the queue
with her basket full of dreams
In control of the boy,
patiently waiting her turn
to be scanned and judged.
She was about my height
with black trousers and a coloured top,
she wasn't bending forward
but had a ten inch gap
between the top and her jeans.
And in the gap was visible
the briefest of black briefs
with a thong that deeply cut
between the cheeks painfully.
With a masochistic tension,
it had the potential to bifurcate,
to cut her in two.
You could see the stubble fuzz
on them like a peach.
I suppose the view was worth a pound
but was it worth the pain?
and in the context of a bargain shop.
It was unsettling for the men
and half the women.
But then again perhaps we need disturbing

Snapshots

The wedding day broke perfectly
with the crash of doom,
The rain was sheeting down
like day one of the flood.
She opened her eyes though
she hadn't been asleep
and groaned, it was an omen
for her doubts about the man.
He opened his eyes and moaned,
two hours of sleep was all he'd had
for he had done his duty last night.
He'd drunk and leered and talked
the staggering night away
It was an omen, he'd talked to God
for two hours and he heard that God
wasn't pleased and was pissing on the day
For breakfast she had tea and toast
and talked to dad about the day, and
the dress was lovely but had cost too much
Dad's speech would be the death of him.
He skipped breakfast and focussed
on dimming the light
through half closed eyes
and sunglasses
Traditionally, she was late at the church
which didn't help him settle
his mind and stomach for the day
The light shone through the stained glass
bilious on the tense faces of an alien
wedding crowd from Ruritania
The men were dressed for Ascot
or a smiling butlers convention
His suit was stiff and unforgiving
his stomach rumbled in the silence
and then the organ blasted and he thought
how did this happen, where did it all go wrong.
With a rustle she was beside him
and his heart skipped a beat
She looked superb, so calm and happy
and the dress was worth every penny

He realised how lucky he was
to have conned her so far
And she was thinking
of the new life to come
and their new life to come
And with her new name
and personality,
everything was new.
The service was a blur
except the kiss at the end
They both felt sick
and smiled a lot in the sunshine
after the rain, God was smiling.
The meal and tears and speeches
wandered on fleshing out their stories
on the bone.
The next stop would be
the buffet dinner disco dance
Where everyone got merry
in a melancholy way, the talking time
of looking back and forward sadly.
For time was passing and everyone
was looking older, even the children
were children no more.
They left at nine in a tin canned
graffiti car, in the rain again,
for the airport and a resort
they couldn't spell,
literacy and geography
were not their strong points.
They would return to penury
paying for the house and kids.

Mappa Io

My failures boundarise my life
The promontories and peninsulars
show the shape of me
with no pattern or design.
All it shows is the endeavour
to shape the quagmire into meaning.
The pathways are arrow straight
over the edge of the end
My thoughts are lemming like
And rush to futility,
So that the shape is meaningless
The carbuncle defines me
and the paths criss-cross
Building a net to trap me in.
Sometime the way is quicksand
So I flounder in the morass
and drown in my plans.
The shape isn't ugly, it's typical of me
Showing the clown, and the farce
The joke that is my life.
So that I smile and straiten up the coast,
And stitch the scars together in an
Abstract tapestry
of self inflicted wounds.
I don't know where I'm going
But I can see where I've been.
The map is my best creation
And so I have to laugh or cry,
And so I choose to laugh.

The Bargain

All hail to you, My Lord,
show yourself to me
That I may see the glory of your face
and speak to you.
O Lord hear my prayer
for I am weak,
and you are most powerful.
You see the wonders of your world,
The silk shotten scintillation of the dawn
The deep imperial purple throb of dusk
Lapis lazuli and pearl
Treasures in the formless deeps
Golden ones in dance,
Diamonds frosted on the wintered trees
Silver cymbals clash in light
The cities sweat blood
The beauty in the blood,
beauty in decay,
The pain that comes with power,
The silence that comes with death.
For you are mighty,
and I am poor and nothing.
Grant my fervent wish
that I may feel the riches of desire
and be fulfilled in ecstasy.
And bathe in glory,
And stand before you
And be valued
And be worthy
For in your iron gaze is truth.
Give me the gift,
And seal the bargain with a kiss.
So that Lord Lucifer
You may claim my soul

Reminisce

Oh!, my doppelganger how I miss
you showing me the way
to the land I lost
And never found
again I lost the map
of treasure islands lying
there. There you said
the treasure lies in chests
and belly's to trap me in
and empty of lies I made
up in my verdigris
certainty
Oh! My salvation comes
no more the wisdom pure
and simple is the way
to peace of mind
less I forget your love
of life, joyful spirit
is no more to guide
me in the mess
Uncertain and unsure
I'm lost in the ash
blowing in the breeze
of time remembered
Evermore.

The Coming

I am an alien from a distant land
evicted from dark to burning light
naked and alone
When I came through the wall
and breathed the sizzling spitting air
and sucked in life and pain
I kicked and screamed at the injustice
The bitter cold air scalded my blameless skin,
I was innocent.
The sound was loud within my head
and my sight, bright and terrible
I closed my eyes and cried.
My first sound was the crying howl
alerting the universe that I was here
for I was born to rage
Loud was my protest to the watching world
my skin as raw and tender as a wound
for I was born in blood
My time had started soft with desire
and now I desired all and everything
in my troubled time.
More than anything to come I was tested
and I had rode the riotous wave
fit training for the rest
My world was unknowing and unknown
a joke, a riddle without an answer
the question without end.
Alone I demanded satisfaction for the hurt
my wail to God went unanswered
forever more I was alone.

The Field

The summer sun shone on the meadow
in full bloom.
the grasses thigh high and golden,
a whirling burnished starburst,
The myriad pulsating seething life of it,
Oh measure me the joy of it.!
The flowers had erupted
frothing through the golden haze,
rampant in their brazen colours,
Jewels in a golden crown.
The laid back breeze touched them
and they bobbed their heads
swirling in the sea of grass.
The hazy lazy day was hot and calm
and bathed the ground in languor
The meadow was busy with life
Butterflies fluttered carelessly
In ambling amateur flight
a moving copy of the flowers
The drone tumble, bumble flower stealers scout by at earnest workmanlike labour
gathering the harvest. before the frost
Birds were busy in their singing work
flooding the meadow with delight.
And the silent swallows winged
swift and low across the grass
The fox in the long grass was resting,
hiding from man and the sun
waiting for dusk and the hunters moon.
The field was warm and scented
Dusty, sleepy, comfortable and safe
It was paradise in a day.
The man looked down, it was good
and had always been so.

The Crow

It hit the ground with a thwack
and strutted, waddled to the prey,
It waited for its mate to land
they always hunt in pairs.
Black as sin and just as powerful
it had a hammer head
it had the evil yellow eye
and a beak to disembowel
or pick out eyes.
The perfect butcher machine,
efficient as a guillotine.
The Gestapo bird.
Before us it was here,
Old as England
And part of the landscape
Cackling as it sits upon the bough
Shitting bile upon the world.
It had the intelligence,
It had the confidence
of one who rules the wood
with the swagger of a king
and knowledge of its power.
it looked the part,
designed for malevolence,
not by God but by Hieronymus Bosch
or Hitchcock.
It had to be black and have a cry
to curdle milk
no other colour would do,
the witches partner
in the dark, waste land,
the land of malcontent.

Yesterday

I'd lost yesterday and half today
by looking in the glass to find the answer,
no, to find the question
And now I felt awful bad after the night
the staggershanking, rolling roaring
the freedom of it all night,
now comes the prison of the day.
I felt awful bad on the fuzzy bleeding floor
and knew the punishment to come,
the pain of loathing reality,
the vomit yellow, the green piss, and purple shit.
I wonder what yesterday will bring,
my life is full of unknown yesterdays
Where I spend money like there's no tomorrow,
because there isn't.
I look in the mirror at the crumpled suit
half off, half on the crumpled me
We suit each other perfectly, I look the part
for I play the part of pissed up poet,
a shambling Dylaness excuse without the talent
The mirror doesn't lie, showing the day   that got away in perfect truth, if I can bare to look.
I drink to not remember me, I had a name once,
but now I do forget, which is some sort of success.
My rumpled mind is focussed on getting through
to the next drink painlessly, you know.
I've not got to the bottom of it yet,
when I shall be on meths
and sleep on a bench, wrapped in paper,
a parcel for God to unwrap in the end.

The House

The ghost wasn't in the house,
the ghost was the house.
It waits in the dark lane,
and the stillness in the air
is perfect for the pain.
it waits the time to come,
it has the time, it has eternity.
It breathes and sighs in and out,
creaks and groans out and in.
Its windoweyes are open to the night,
it sees the wicked in the wind,
and smells the fear in the fog.
It senses the coming of the victim
with baleful relish for the victory,
When the innocent is sucked dry
when all is weighed and the mind is cracked
LIke the mirror in the dusty hall
and madness walks the corridors
In soft carpet slippers, whispering.
The garden looks in silence on the scene,
Icy cold indifferent,
and the bat is hanging on the bough
viewing the upside down.
The merciless stars look down
And the moon shines on the frosted carpet,
silent as the grave.

Sizemograf

The erthquake xploded in his chest
justafter the litening bolt nife
peirsed his between the ribus
gowting the blud fromout him
The payn it was considerable,
his nees crumpled and he fell
like a bilding with its base blown out.
He dropped, slowly rolling
In slomotion he hit the ground
and bounced into the gutter.
The bottle skitterattled from him fast.
one arm was cross his chest
Fingering the wound
the other flung out wide,
a broken crucifix.
He lay lazily and bled along the cobbles
on his bak oozing his life way   contemplating the moon
and called for his mom.
He herd them run, and each one
kiked him skilfully as he went past.
The silence after they had gone was sereen.
He felt so week he cryed from siteless eyes
He felt the cold start at his toes
and rise in paynless tide,
his site had gon, he was still
and he cud feel deth
claym his body bit by bit
easily, efficiently and
with fulfilment claym its own.
And he did breeth no more,   silence came bak to the street.

He's Buildin A Car In The Shed

He's buildin a car in the shed,
He wanted a challenge you know
And fortune it favours the brave.
So he'd stopped work at fifty
For arthritic reasons, relaxed
and never looked back.
The shed was a toolroom you know,
equipped with all comforts and tools
with a miller. a Welder and lathe
And on the walls neatly arrayed
every single tool you could imagine
and some you couldn't
From tubes he's welded a chassis
And designed it as he goes along
from his factory craft and some credit
For he knows what he's doing you know,
Its not just a pie in a sky
He's bought in the engine and seats
The wheels, the tyres and the lights
And the rest he is making himself.
It's looking a bit like a Fangio car
crossed with a hill climbing racer
It looks fast and is fast he says,
One hundred and ten in the shade
He's creating a car from his soul,
A work of art fashioned from love
In the shed he is building a car
And its hard and its true and its red
It rides on a tightrope of doubt
It rides on the edge of defeat
The purpose for all his tomorrows
Built on his yesterday dreams
staring silence with a cup of tea
Zen hermit with a welding torch.
He's buildin desire in his shed
and it's totally his own you know,   made with passion and an oily rag
the triumph, the glory all in a shed
So the shed, although rather large
Is beginning to get rather full
the trouble is getting it out.

He'll dismantle the end of the shed,
carefully roll the masterpiece out.
it's going to be tight allright
And will moderately damage the garden
So he wont tell the wife
that a tree and some shrubs have to go.
Though being a woman she knows
and plays him like a fish on a hook,
so although he will bluster and shout
he hasn't a chance, the list's ready made out
He'll be paying for this a very long time

Blood Song

- In pleinsong do I whet the air
- with the sharpness of my tale,
- about the coming of the sword
- to our land at lambing time.
- They came from out the mist and marsh,
- They came from out the biting east
- They came to cleanse us to the grave
- strange people with another tongue,
- with outlandish battle cries, fearful
- with war song and with heartlessness,
- They scorched and scarred the land
- and butchered as they went.
- The frighteners carried death
- upon their blackened metal shields
- seeking for the lifeblood in the mire
- so that mud became russet
- Our fields and pastures now are gone
- Our livestock now are in the woods
- where so are we, animal with beast
- and they delight to hunt us both
- to blood us for their bloody sport.
- Only wild dogs roam the empty streets
- And so they've taught us bitterly
- the lessons of outlaw revenge,
- That they have fired us in the crucible
- and tempered our steel to diamond bright.
- So that the frighteners now affright
- and look behind them as they march,
- Their moon is waning on the rim.
- They rule the day, we claim the night
- and many a knight ends in the night and slit the throat with skilful ease,
- One for one the body count is par
- but we have our God and hatred
- on the righteous scything side.
- Now the devil fears the blood law,
- Now do machines rust in their tracks
- and with our right arm of justice
- we will kill death and the devil
- and revenge cleanse our holy land

- We sing our songs and sacrifice
- ourselves upon our blessed earth
- I come to speak and write the wrongs
- We will survive. By god we serve.

Flash

- I wish I could download
- Adobe Flash ten,
- I've tried for a month
- in all types of ways
- and all types of positions
- both Buddhist and Zen
- Each time I switch on
- I try without hope
- I glance at him sideways
- and try to creep up
- very nonchalantly in a carefreedomly lope

- I've shouted and pleaded
- and whispered the fact
- That my desire for the programme for downloading
- programmes is uploading my brain and making me cracked
- he just won't obey me,
- he acts like he's deaf,
- Or foreign, or stupid,
- by refusing to play
- We're just not connecting,
- he thinks he's the chef
- he says that he's done it
- and smirks in my face
- But there's nothing on desktop
- to show that he's there
- It's a mystery for me,
- A mind blowing case
- He plays the game smoothly
- and holds all the aces,
- he is dealing duds to me
- jack after bloody joker
- All I get is the low ones,
- he gets all the faces
- I know that he's after me
- With all of his might
- Just because I'm paranoid
- Doesn't prove me wrong
- He's planning, and he's scheming

- But I'm fighting the good fight
- On bended knee I pray to him softly through the gate video
- I have the end, pull out the plug, let me have closure by murder
- Let me have liberty, him or me, one of us will have to go.

It's A Small World

We live in Lilliput
But we don't know it.
Tribes of dwarves, elves, gnomes,
The little people
Swarm the land in self important ease
Strutting on the stage
In mutual appreciation
Of mutual mediocrity
Midgets measure midgets
Against their own small selves
Valuing by column inch,
And appreciating bloody fame
For all is bloody style
The dunghill quivers with life
And Since everyone is in it
They can't recognise crap
So they spin their threads from it
And weave their clothes
On the loom of platitude
It's not the poor that talk the talk,
But the establishment, the elite
Who talk to themselves,
Who live in Lilliputs,
but with gates,
Segregating the rich
For the rich are always with us.
Self satisfied and smug
Wake up you bastards
and try harder,
At least I know my worth,
I'm dross talking to myself.
Better to fail in glory
Than succeed in balderdash
Fight for the light,
Breach the walls of the asylum
And let the sunshine in,
And let the giants in.
If we are in God's image`
If this is the best that God can do,
Then God help God.

Lifetime

In the corner of a dusky, dusty room
sits a child alone absorbed and chatting, laughing
to the listening ones.
Tousled and pock marked
with playtime dirt,
Unkempty but lifefull
the debris of the toy box
litters the floor
and boxes it in,
the black button eyes
are shining out the gloom,
The faces smile in confidence.
It grasps its foot
and counts its toes
and wonders why.
It rapid gabbles to the crew
with half made words
that only they will really know,
about the day and all the world
to pick and mix.
The stories tumble out unbid
The setting sunlight catches
specks of floating dust,   and majic is in the air
Three summers full of life
have filled its world to brim
with secrets to whisper
and stories to shout and share
around the gang tonight
It is the hour before sleep time,
the drowsy best time of the day.
The light is less than light,
night and dreams are creeping in.
It finds its trusty friend
propped up, watching and waiting
for they always sleep together,
neither could sleep alone.

The Irish Boy

I read Brendan Behan today,
'Borstal Boy' it was, and o by God
to write like that.
The words just firing off the pen,
fuelled by Guinness no doubt
and wasted by it as well.
The surely God gifted talent
proves God must be a brewer
or why make the stuff at all, at all.
It is the oil, the lubrication
of the cogs, the gears spinning
in the whirring mind
So that the mode is fast and free.
He had a pugilistic face squashed
and with the nose flattened
in the fighting lifesome game.
He could have dropped me
with one flat hand slap
and he could write me under the
table
with a poem or two.
I think I like him for his honesty
and his inbred hatred of me,
being ironic English,
and his fight against fame
which destroyed him in the end.
An urban peasant lad confident
And cocksure, still blowing
the sparks of a fag end of life.
Like all rebels he was spoilt
by success and finished by   the establishment
Still I think I'd go his way
if I could have one week
of his eye and his voice.

Sleep Time

I had a strange long dream last night,
Initially based in the shop,
on a busy hustling bustling satisfying day,
It was a daydream.
And later in a room with French windows
at a function with food, music
it was peopled with family and friends,
a party or celebration.
In the first part Charles was very unpleasant,
which was unusual.
And in the second the room was full and overflowed
through the windows.
It was a warm night and an enjoyable occasion,
the wine flowed
the dancing and the conversation flowed
I knew everyone.
It was late when I left and walked my way home
in the warm night air,
Thinking of the happy time, bemused and happy,
but on the way
I was downed and as I lay on the ground
I wrote in troubled blood
"I LOVE YOU ALL"........how strange.

Superday

I walk the aisle religiously
With head bowed to the script
To read the rewards for tomorrow
and the record for today.
And images of the golden hours
The voices from above, they talk to me
I walk in dreamland through the throng
For I am known and valued in the scheme
For I believe devoutly in the scheme,
The company of serving men
Who feed and satisfy our hunger
They have their standards, and they work to it,
The golden harvest of the uniform.
The lady with delight feeds us the truth
They believe in the spreading of the word
To the world, one day we will be one.
They feature on the TV everyday
And advertise the coming goodtime
So that there is one word and it is theirs
The sweetness and the bitter
The blessed trinity, two for one for one
All for one and one for all
And the payment at the end.

Passion Flower

My love is like the morning star,
my love is like the rose.
The sunset glow is not so fair
she lights the world candescant.
Her name I scratch on every car,
I burn the blessed name in fire
it runs in blood down watching walls.
She calls the night stream passion
that doubts me in the dark
black rain will be upon me
on the sanctity of sin.
Sugar sweet's the kisses
from the cherry loaded lips.
She is the witch of desire
that sings the song
to kill the heart with longing
and cry the everlasting tears.
The blossom blooms within the night,
the canker spreads my brain,
She speaks in wantonness
the honey words that trap me
and bind me to the dreamtime.
She's my delight and my despair
she's all to me and nothing
From all women I separate
from all women my love is lent
And light on her alone.

The Woman

The rain was falling gently on her,
but she stood her ground
and gazed upwards at the tree.
On one side, the bark was rough and gnarled
the blood was running down it
in rivulets
and collected at the bottom
in puddles.
Her hand was touching the stake
for support and connection
with the man,
and the blood ran cross her hand
warm and slow.
Soft and low was her speech
as she did kiss the blood.
She wept and her tears ran
in couple with the rain,
combining, for the world was crying.
She bared her head
and rent and tore her clothes
in the unforgiving rain.
Gazing on the body, she knelt.
and then he spoke,
and then he cried,
and then the storm broke
On the hill. she still looked up
and blessed the storm
to wash away the pain.
After the end, she walked back
down the hill in silence
holding her mother to her chest.

Plainsong

Everyone is a poem
the best are songs,
we needs a singer
to serenade
and unlock the story in
our tightshut shell
it is the key.
So that the wonder
of the tale
becomes a thrilling
we can see
We stamp the ground
and dance the rhythm
of the story told.
It needs a poet teller
worthy of the life
to tell the ribbon winding
through the piece
and tell the truth
comic, sad, or terrible.
Each person a villain,
thief or saint,
a hero or a nobody.
We're told the legends,
who have slain our fears
and live again for ever
With the power of their name,
with the power of the word.
Ten thousand years
we're told the song
around the campfire.
And put on the mask
of animal and sniff the air
to steal the song
to tell the magic to the air
and to the dark silent tribe,
the tribes of the horse
and the swan
and the roaring bear.
For the time come,
when the glory speaks,
when the Shaman speaks.

Primavera

Spring has sprung
the trap of winter
snaps the icicle falls
as the water of life
and life comes back
to back the arcing sun
in the melting foggy dew
hibernations over
and the young and new
stretches itself
towards the light
the creation begins
again every year
in sizzling colours
yellow, white and blue
bedeck the bough
and the land erupts
with spouts of life
the land is busy
with the greening
hurry of the year
and winter is forgot
the tree remembers
to cascade the blossom
on the bristling branch
for The first few bees
and in the misty, sodden morn
the sheep are dropping
new lambs for the eastertime
a new bright day is born
to shine upon the year
and every time
a new Eden is come

Day Room

The residential caring
is in malodorous full swing.
The bright eyed ladies
don't move much
but watch the morn
pass by like yesterday.
And wait the coming of the lunch,
being the Friday menu
for it is Friday,
and lunchtime.
The staff are kind and considerate
in a defeated way,
for they are the ones
who recognise the sameness
of the dreaming days.
They're not paid much
for heroism beyond the call,
and there are many calls
to service the day
With love and talk and biscuits
Once upon a long time ago
the old ones ran the world
and skipped easily through life
with confidence
in their modern ways
Now the husks give hints
of what they were 50 years ago
when they built there lives
on dreams.
But the ring has run it's race
back to the beginning,
from child to child
and the memories are going
back to back to the beginning
on a glitching loop.
There are tears sometimes
when they remember
or forget.
They don't want much
just safety and a cuddle.

Silent Night

The rain had finished
freshing the ground,
and each leaf glistened
in the nightime air.
The raindrops rolling
off the hedgerows,
the puddles quivered
in the moonlight
and In the bracken a body,
a silhouette stirred.
Two eyes reflected the moon
silence blobbed the land,
the games afoot.
A moth was flying to the moon
in bumbling, humming flight
and fragrance tipped the air
with promise of a kill.
The head is turned towards the breeze
and samples the night,
it reads the space intently
and feels the life
Flexing, moving, dancing and glowing,
life is steaming in the night.
quietly the living move,
for silence is golden
and noise is dangerous.
in the damp, dark wood
the feathered fronds of grass
whisper in the breeze.
Slowly, it moves it's body
to pivot to the sound
that needs inspection,
it focusses on nothing
but the sound,
it moves forward
in the direction
slowly and surely
and holds its breath.
The bright sky spangled
shows it perfectly
in the dead of night,
And then it leaps.

Dust

Bethlehem is down and done,
the craters mark the bombing run.
The houses lopside to the ground,
silence is the only sound,
down the road to Samarkand
the mirage bubbled on the sand,
the white bones glisten where they fall
and Babylon's beyond recall.
Let us know where blooms the rose
now death is scattered with the blows,
where flies the cherry on the bough?,
the oxen lies beside the plough.
Gone is the dove and the lamb
and the sacrificial ram,
the flowers bloom not on the hill
and the tribes are born to kill.
Jerusalem layered stone on stone
vultures picking bone on bone
the lake of Galilee is rust
and Rome is levelled in the dust.
In Gaza eyeless sockets look
upon the peoples of the book,
the waters poisoned in the well
the stoneground is as hot as hell.
The frozen nights are feared and wrong
the bone dry days last far too long.
Tattered banners limply fly
above the husks of Tripoli,
loud is the silence cross the land,
soft is the war cry of the damned
Christian, Hindu, Muslim, Jew must
Lie together in the dust.
The end has come, writ in red
God is dead.

Notes On A Cataract

I write this one eyed,
a cyclops scrivener,
a one dimensional poem
And a descant on infirmity.
About the humour of faults,
for isn't there black comedy
about a deaf Beethoven
singing to himself.
And blind Milton
talking in the dark,
poor mad Dadd
hearing voices in his head
all the stuff of legend
and of mirth.
How did Milton cross the road
without being run down
by retreating Cavaliers?,
the world must have seemed
very flat, including Emma
to asymmetric Nelson.
Quasimodo couldn't hear
the bells, only feel
the vibrations in the air.
Sure Boswell and Pepys
were always on top
of the ladies.
Would they have been great
without their faults?
I've had a bypass
and a cancer, without them
would I be so wonderful?.
Talent is forged
in the crucible
of our defects.
Pain concentrates
the mind to the importance
of imperfections.
And so I think
to improve my art
I should break my leg.

Bar Room Talk

Depression?
I'll tell you what
depression is,
it's when the glass
is only half full
of nothing.
I'll tell you what
ecstasy is,
it's when the glass
is half full
of everything.
Which proves the point
that we need
smaller glasses,
for to fill them up
would make us drunk
on nothing,
or everything.
But definitely drunk

Ressurection

Two miles down we sweat,
We think of death and dark,
we think of light and life
and blue and green
and dream of songs
and children, wives and mistresses
and kneel and pray
to god with tears of hope.
We sweat because we're near to hell,
black and hot and dirty
in the devils hand,
deep in the devils hole.
He smiles upon us, his subjects
and then turns up the heat
and bends the roof, squeezing out
the light and life and hope.
Compressed we crouch
praying to the devil and to god,
we're not alone, they keep us company.
For we are sinners and deserve our fate,
we shout and plead up
the narrow tube of life
bringing the sweet air
to this stinking sweating hole.
Now the stone is rolled back
and Holy Mary leads us home
to our coloured heaven.
Now we are rising, one by one
segmented like a snake.,
The snake is ending and I am the tail
reborn again I rise, for I am famous
as the last

Voyager

Hoist the sail and see the shore
of dreamy neverland no more.
The crocodile is dead and gone
so we shall hunt a snarkothon
within the far off land of nod
where many a coppers name is plod,
in pirate treasure island
The colander is leaking fast,
the albatross tied to the mast,
overboard he'll have to go.
The beaver will have to row
for none of us can swim a stroke,
we haven't slept since we awoke
like leathery Rip Van Winkle,
We're steering by blue moon tonight,
the cow has jumped it in a fright
and down among the crew there sits
a hatter who has lost his wits,
The dormouse sleeps sound and sure
and dreams of treacle clear and pure
with Paddington
A mermaid swims 'long the boat
and urges us to sink or float.
Upon the prow stands King Canute
his jester plays upon his flute,
up to their knees in froth and bubble
and to their necks in trial and trouble.
The rats have left us long ago.'
We'll have to beach upon the strand,
the walrus leading to the sand
singing to the oysters there
sea shanties of a jolly fare
to keep their spirits in fine fettle
hot bathing in a copper kettle
to make them clean as clams should be.
The shipwreck is upon us now,
and most are clinging to the prow,
Captain Hook is standing proud
upon the deck and shouting loud
'women, kids and captains first'.
We slosh and squelch fearing the worst
but at ten inch deep we couldn't drown if we tried.

Schooltime

The day was overcast and bitter.
He spat upon the hard frozen ground
The kid was out for devilment,
he wiped the dewdrop from his nose
with his sleeve and looked around.
He'd pinched everything out
the wrecked car on the corner,
The only thing left to take
were the wheels.
He'd begged the apple cores
off his mates and was full.
He filled his pockets, like David,
with smooth throwing stones
and openly pee'd against the wall
trying to beat his altitude record,
and decided about the day.
He thought school would be best,
it was empty but the heat was on
so he could thieve in comfort.
His Dad was lost in the war
as was the town,
so when he left home he was free   for anything he fancied,
the only rule was don't get caught.
And he liked to be alone when on a job,
no kids to look after or to share,
children were always a problem.
He pulled up his socks and his collar
and picked his way through the rubble
circling towards the school silently
as a good thief should.
Some crows were picking over
something dead raucously,
the only sound except the wind.
The school wasn't secure,
It was child's play,
And he played the game,   he broke a window at the back,
(the alarm was broke) Inside   it was as silent as a morgue,
but his heart was beating loud,
the corridors were hushed
and the hall echoed to his shout,

the classrooms were spooky
he fancied ghosts would walk at night.   He went to the kitchen for some food,
not too much, he'd come back again,
found a coat that would do him fine.   then had a shit and a wash in the warmth.
He didn't vandalise, that was for kids
and had a sleep in the corner
with his back against the wall
like Wyatt Earp, by a radiator.
And dreamt of his Dad.
When he woke up two thin dogs
were staring at him, they were small
so he chased them off with his stones.
He went back to the kitchen,
and found a good long stabbing knife,
just in case.
Got some sausages out the freezer
and burnt them up in a frying pan,
he was good at cooking,   ate half and kept the rest for later.
It was time to go, dusk was falling
and the curfew would be on,
he looked around to see he'd left no clue
that he'd been there, he was smart.
And went towards his home in the gloom
with some food for the family,
he was the breadwinner now.
There were no street lights
so to move was hard in the black out,
It was the dangerous dark.
but his big black coat was warm
and he had the cats eyes of the young,
yes he could see in the dark.
Soon he was at the hole that was home,
but no one was there except the cat
and for the first time he cried.
Now he really was alone,
The kid wept.
He'd burn the school tomorrow.

Midsummer Night-------2

Masturbate your life away pigsticker,
You are dreaming of the waste
We will call you when we want
And shagdance you through your life
And you will ask for more.
Hear the breeze and sigh the sigh
Lie your life in beds of fear
who are you?
We know you are nothing
Fly the night and hide the day
The moon is garlanded with blood
And you are riding the nightmare
Just to please us
you are a puppet on the stage
And we pull the strings of madness
You dangle o'er the darkling pit
And sway in the breeze of time
A clown in hell
The grimace is a leering grin
The face is made up for the play
We are the masters of the day
And screw you to the fiery door
With bands of steel.
You'll lie in quicklime for eternity
Laughing at the theatre of the mad.

Prophet

The smile says it all,
not so much a smile
but a rictus grin
which will still be there
at his final game.
The gypsy life for him,
wandering and wondering
always moving, moving
like the flying Dutchman
or the wandering Jew.
Each mile a pilgrimage
with the backbreak
of his spendthrift triumph
The more he pays
The more he owes
Homeless in a thousand rooms
he's a five star
and first class.
The man of peace
that killed a country dead
Wary of his friends,
fearful of his foes
Frightened of the truth
he rides the nightmare
that he made
He rides the merry-go-round
famously and tanned
Watching the fairgrounds
friendless rides,
a world without end
Smiling to the jostling throng
hr acts the part of statesman
Wishing he was him
on the whirling stage.
The greeks had a word for it - tragedy.
He feels the hate of some,
I feel the sorrow. the pity of it all,
For his greatest weakness is his strength
Vanity of vanities,
All is vanity.

Lifetime

In the corner of a dusky, dusty room
sits a child alone absorbed and chatting, laughing
to the listening ones.
Tousled and pock marked
with playtime dirt,
Unkempt but lifefull
the debris of the toy box
litters the floor
and boxes it in,
the black button eyes
are shining out the gloom,
The faces smile in confidence.
It grasps its foot
and counts its toes
and wonders why.
It rapid gabbles to the crew
with half made words
that only they will really know,
about the day and all the world
to pick and mix.
The stories tumble out unbid
The setting sunlight catches
specks of floating dust,   and majic is in the air
Three summers full of life
have filled its world to brim
with secrets to whisper
and stories to shout and share
around the gang tonight
It is the hour before sleep time,
the drowsy best time of the day.
The light is less than light,
night and dreams are creeping in.
It finds its trusty friend
propped up, watching and waiting
for they always sleep together,
neither could sleep alone.

Pirouette

You can't hear them laughing
in your sleep,
Only the crying cuts the ice
skating in your dreams
on the edge
of breaking through
to the dark underland.
The thin sheet creaking
With the weight of cold comfort.
Whose down there in the deep?
waiting to destroy you're smile
silent and ancient and patient.
You skim the edges of your mind
in beautiful filigree patterns,
only the speed keeps you up,
you must never stop.,
stopping means you stop
The monsters of the deep
are sweeping subs
with mouths agape
waiting for the thaw
that thins the ice.
The surface is a two way mirror,
on top reflects your day,
below the madness lurks
in the upside down.
Where the silver moon is queen
and reigns in lunacy.
Keep awake in wide eyed innocence,
for to dream is to scream,
you'll hear it in your sleep,
Sleep no more.

Fireside

The winter is the killing time
for the old and poor,
iron cold and shattering
comes through the shuttered door,
The dark on dark advances
one step at a time
remorseless and unwanted
Fogging the rooms with rime.
The clock is ticking softly
in the silent hall
measuring out the season
of goodwill and death to all.
The killing fields are iron hard
the lanes are rutted black
the frost bites at the branches
the snow's deep on the track
The rabbits in its burrow,
the fox is in its den
they sleep or starve or die
within the frozen fen.
To children a wonderland
of beauty, black and white
adventures on the way to play
in air's silver sparkling bite.
The landscape's drained of colour,
the pools are made of glass
mists are shrouding fields
and frost silvers the grass.
A woodcut world of silent
beauty grips the land
and jewels the cobwebs
with its frosted hand
Snow is falling, large and soft
hushing the world,
and crunching footsteps
crushing the world
the short days wither
into the cold dark night
the iron grip is squeezing
out the bitter days light.

Coldsleep

I'll feel the sun no more
when I am dead,
no cast of shadow fore me
down the path,
The taste of wine
and drunkenness is gone
to stone cold sober.
the breeze upon my cheek
is stopped in calm,
The warm kisses
are for the living,
this is the stillness
of the lonesome dead.
Lying there alone
upon the slab
cold as marble
soft as loam
In my six foot hole
of dark nothing.
The marker stone
above my head
etching my life
of memories soon forgot.
As the ring of
black clad witnesses
round the cask of me.
The churchyard crow
watches for the crowd to go
to gorge on well fed worms
This is the long sleep
of the judged.
The sun is setting
on my life and me
with long black shadows
pointing eastwards
to the cold.

Atonement

I am my brother's keeper
and I keep him safe and sound.
Inviolate and crystal clear
in my glistening mind's eye.
I remember more
and know him more
and understand more myself.
I value evermore his soul
that lives on in my memory,
a precious hoard of stories
good and bad, but surely good.
A golden treasure of his life
Deep buried in my head
Inside my head he lives,
each day an adventure
to be desired
and eager for the taste of life.
All nights an experience
to be explained
feeling the pain and joy.
Whence comes another
like him now?.
A comfortable man
untroubled by the troubles
of our storm tossed life,
right as rain upon the earth
I am haunted by the ghost
in every day
we are fashioned by our lives
and he improved on me,
He had the love, I had the hate
and I loved to hate.
He had the light of life
that shone upon us all.
He was too good to live
and so he had to die
I am bitter to my bone
and bear witness to the truth,
whilst I live, so does he.

Saturnalia

The pub was rocking to the sound
of the New Years stomp,
The drunks and tarts
were swaying with eyes closed
to the band playing loud.
The band was loud
because the band was drunk.
To talk you had to shout
in each others ear
the usual banal wisdom
of their crowded lonely lives,
and cry a bit about the life
that got away.
It was full and took an hour
to get a drink
and pay whatever they said
who's counting?.
Behind the bar they looked out tiredly
upon the sea of faces,
the noisy swirling sea of humanity
that wanted to have a good time
no matter what the pain.
Soon they would break through to tomorrow
when tomorrow is today,
Tomorrow they would look on it
and say they didn't remember much

Fireworks

It was raining hard
and they marched
sullenly through the mud
along the ditch.
Silently the squad moved
in the hiss of the rain,
they were moving to a plan
dreamed up behind the lines,
a nightmare plan.
The squad was a family,
as each one cared
for the friend in front
each one a hero in the push
in the dark
fighting for the right
to fall for family and home,
Brothers in arms
they were the lads
the frightened squad,
crouching in the mist of rain
Each one a frightened hero
in the push, in the dark
Then the hell began
with light and sound and smell.
The flares showed up the field
and them brighter than the day.
The big guns 'KERRUMPED'
and shot a plume of death into the air,
the little guns buzzed and howled
like angry fiery wasps
and where they stung
a boy dropped
covering them in war.
The ground shuddered
with the agony, and smoked with rage
The smell was cordite and wet death
The storm of war
was raining blood upon them
in the poppy fields
Red on red.

Printed in the United States
By Bookmasters